DATE DUE

FINDING HER WAY HOME

**Center Point
Large Print**

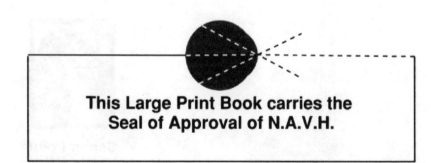

**This Large Print Book carries the
Seal of Approval of N.A.V.H.**

FINDING HER WAY HOME

Linda Goodnight

CENTER POINT LARGE PRINT
THORNDIKE, MAINE

The text of this Large Print edition is unabridged.
In other aspects, this book may vary
from the original edition.
Printed in the United States of America.
Set in 16-point Times New Roman type.

ISBN: 978-1-60285-717-9

Library of Congress Cataloging-in-Publication Data

Goodnight, Linda.
    Finding her way home / Linda Goodnight. — Large print ed.
       p. cm.
    ISBN 978-1-60285-717-9 (alk. paper)
    1. Single mothers—Fiction. 2. Oklahoma—Fiction. 3. Large type books. I. Title.
PS3557.O5857F56 2010
    813'.54—dc22
2009045406

If I say "surely the night will cover me,"
even the night will be light around me.
The darkness is not dark to You,
and the night shines as the day.

—*Psalms* 139:11–12

One of my personal heroes is my daughter, Sundy Goodnight, whose heart is bigger than the sun and who has truly forsaken all to follow the call of the Lord. For her work with Stop Child Trafficking Now, a humanitarian group determined to end the sexual sale of children, as well as for the hundreds of hours of counseling she's done with broken young women, particularly rape and abuse victims. Her knowledge and understanding of a woman's psychological function after sexual assault was invaluable in the writing of this book.

Chapter One

Cheyenne Rhodes had hoped if she drove far enough she could outrun the darkness. But six hundred miles and counting had done nothing to shake the brooding anxiety that overtook her one unspeakable night a year ago. In her own garage. With a known criminal. And no help in sight.

She circled her head to loosen the knot in her shoulders and shook off the images flickering through her mind like a bad action movie. It was over. He was dead. She had to forget what had happened and start her life again. Somehow.

She shot a glance at the map opened on the seat beside her. Her destination, a small Oklahoma town, couldn't be too much farther.

She gave a derisive snort. The town was more like a hiding place than a destination. A place far, far from Colorado. A place where her face and name would not be known, would not be plastered on the front pages of the newspaper, where no one cared what she'd done or suffered that one terrible night.

She clicked on the radio, hoping for something cheery to dispel the dark thoughts. Up ahead on the side of the road an overturned cardboard box caught her attention. Next to the box was a pair of waddling puppies. Cheyenne groaned and tried not to look.

After a second, her shoulders slumped.

"Sucker," she mouthed, knowing she wasn't heartless enough to pass them by. She pulled to the side of the empty highway and slammed out of her Honda.

The pups toddled toward her, whining softly. Cheyenne clamped down a surge of pity. Hands on her hips, she stared at them. Poor babies wouldn't last long out here on the highway.

"What am *I* gonna do with you? I don't even know where the nearest animal shelter is."

One of the pups climbed onto her shoe and, with his round belly and stubby legs, got stuck on high center. He set up such a fuss of wiggles and whines that the other puppy began to cry louder, too. With a groan of surrender, Cheyenne bent down and lifted the tiny dogs against her cheek. The contact with soft, wiggling puppies brought a smile and for that bit of cheer she owed them. They were mutts, but cute ones with black and white spots and upright ears that flopped forward at the tips. Fat bellies and clean coats indicated they'd been dumped recently.

Puppy dumpers were on her list of low-life scum, though nowhere near the top.

"All right, guys—if you *are* guys—back into

the box you go. I'll give you a lift as far as the next town and then we're done. Deal?"

She had no business taking them in. She didn't want to. But even a tough nut like her couldn't resist a crying puppy.

She crouched beside the box, put the dogs inside and glanced around to be sure no other litter mates had wandered off.

Squinting against the evening sun, she looked down the long stretch of Highway 62 to gauge her location. The pretty road passed verdant rolling hills and distant farmhouses that had grown closer together in the past few miles, a sure sign of approaching civilization. Up ahead, a lazy river flowed beneath an arched bridge, not steel and modern but apparently a throwback to earlier times and made of stone. The foliage increased there, near the river, and the western sunlight glistened on the water. It was a peaceful scene, a scene that beckoned her to explore and relax and forget.

With a huff of annoyance, she shook off the fantastical thoughts. If a change of locales would help her forget, she'd know soon enough. First the puppies.

The town must lie beyond the quaint bridge. Lifting the cardboard box, she stood. As she did, she caught sight of the highway sign just ahead. The shiny green metal beckoned Welcome to Redemption, Oklahoma. Population: 9,425.

Cheyenne squinted hard and read the sign again. She didn't remember seeing that name on the map. But then, she'd chosen her destination by chance. A jab of one finger at the map that was open on the seat beside her and "Bingo!" She'd turned off the interstate and headed down the two-lane toward nowhere. A nowhere with a name like Redemption? The irony wasn't lost on her. She'd driven across three states and wound up in a town called Redemption. Why couldn't the place be called Privacy or Peace? Those were the things she wanted most. Well, those and a good dose of amnesia.

But Redemption? No, she didn't think so. Redemption might be possible for some, but for a woman with her record, it was simply too much to ask.

By the time Cheyenne reached the small town that turned out to be every bit as picturesque as the river bridge, a ball of uncertainty had knotted in her belly. Before last year, she'd never been a worrier, but now paranoia was her constant companion. Had she traveled far enough to outrun her notoriety? Would she find work? Would strangers look at her and know? Would she find someone to take the puppies that had curled into each other and gone fast asleep, their warm smell filling up the car?

As she drove onto the main thoroughfare—a

long street flanked on either side by restored nineteenth-century buildings—she was drawn by a cul-de-sac at the far end where the pavement circled a small parklike area. This became her destination. On one side of the park sat a stately old, buff-stone municipal building with a dozen steps to the top. The police station couldn't be far. Someone here could take custody of the pups.

As she parked and exited the Honda, the box of pups in her arms, she scanned the area. Out of long habit and expert training her brain clicked photos and made an assessment. Little stone pathways led into the middle of the town square to a rustic wishing well. Evergreens, neatly clipped grassy areas and park benches interspersed with long planting boxes made of more stone. From them, squatty pink flowers waved in the soft spring breeze and gave off a pleasant spicy scent.

Nice. Pretty. Like a postcard home.

She sighed. Home was no longer an option.

Up the tree-lined street people moved in and out of the vintage shops, stopping to chat now and then. Car doors slammed. Engines cranked. A blue Buick curved around the circle and parked in front of the *Redemption Register*, a newspaper office.

The town looked peaceful, law-abiding and safe. The tight muscles in her shoulders relaxed.

She started up the sidewalk past a giant green trash receptacle.

"Grab that cartridge, G.I." The booming male voice seemed to come out of nowhere.

Every hair on the back of Cheyenne's neck stood at attention. She whirled and slapped at her side before remembering that her weapon no longer rode there. Frantically searching for the source of the unexpected voice, she spotted a man's head, wearing an old army cap, as he popped up from inside the Dumpster. Another head, this one wearing a headlamp, popped up beside him. The two tossed out several items and then followed them over the side of the receptacle.

Cheyenne stared in stunned amazement, the shiver of fear turning to incredulity. Two grungy old bums Dumpster-diving right here in the middle of town? Where were the cops? Wasn't diving in trash cans against the law in Redemption?

Her frozen stare must have caught the divers' attention. Both studied her with open interest, neither looking the least bit guilty of committing a crime.

"Lookie here, Popbottle," the man with the green army cap said. "We got us a newcomer."

The Popbottle character reached up to flick off his headlamp, his long, skinny neck the likely source of his nickname. "Then I suggest we say hello and find out what's in the box."

The men started forward and Cheyenne unwittingly took a step back, pulse jittery, before she caught herself and stopped. She refused to be afraid of two old men. They were in broad daylight, not in a dark garage with no one near to help.

She gave them her best hard-eyed cop stare. Neither appeared the least bit intimidated.

In amazingly proper English the headlamp man said, "Hello, my dear. Allow me to introduce myself. I'm Ulysses E. Jones, though my compatriots refer to me as Popbottle. And this—" he made a sweeping gesture with a gloved hand "—is my business partner, G. I. Jack. How may we address you?"

Cheyenne opened and closed her mouth twice before deciding that truth was best, though the sentiment had not served her particularly well in the past year. If she stayed in this town, people would ask her name.

"Cheyenne Rhodes." If she sounded defensive, she couldn't help it.

Neither man so much as blinked. A huge relief, though she didn't relax her guard.

The one called Popbottle said, "A pleasure, I'm sure, Miss Cheyenne Rhodes. Pardon my directness but you're looking a bit flummoxed. Can we be of service?"

Only if you can turn back time, she thought bitterly.

13

"Me and Popbottle knows everyone in Redemption," the other one said. "Just ask away. Who you looking for?"

Well, she might as well ask them. In her previous job, street people were often the most useful resource. "I'm trying to find the local police department or an animal control officer."

"Animal control?" The two men edged closer, attention focused on the scratching noise coming from the cardboard box. "What you got there?"

G. I. Jack, his army jacket billowing open, leaned forward. Cheyenne prepared to be overwhelmed by body odor, but the only smell coming from the old bum was that of the French fry container she spied in his shirt pocket. The puppies noticed, too, and tried to crawl up the side of the box, whimpering.

"Lookie here, Popbottle, she's got puppies." Childlike delight filled the man's voice. "Two of 'em."

Popbottle Jones peered into the box as well, one hand holding his miner's lamp in place.

"I found them on the side of the road outside town. Is there an animal shelter here?"

"Yep," G. I. Jack said, brow puckered. "But you can't take 'em there."

"Why not?"

The old man wagged his grizzled gray head back and forth and then made a cutting motion across his throat. "Death row."

14

"Oh." Distress filled her. "Too bad, but I can't keep them."

She knew she sounded heartless and she really wasn't. However, she was a realist. There were, sadly, far too many irresponsible dog owners who allowed dogs to breed and then dumped the pups. The end result was not pretty.

"Why not?" G. I. Jack drew back, his dark, weathered face insulted. "You got something against innocent little dogs? 'Tweren't their fault someone dumped them like . . ." He paused, blinking as if baffled for a comparison. "Well, like stray pups."

"I'm in the process of moving," she said, a little too sharply. "I have no place for dogs." And she didn't want two old bums making her feel bad about it. She had enough guilt without adding puppies to the list.

"No one's blaming you, Miss Cheyenne," Popbottle Jones said in a conciliatory voice. "Dilemmas such as these occur. Allow me a moment to ponder." He tapped the edge of the box, his fingers protruding from the ends of tattered gloves. The puppies stretched up toward him, noses in the air. "Ah, yes. Take them over to Doc Bowman's animal clinic. He'll know what to do."

"Yep. He'll know." G. I. Jack brightened, his old head bobbing again. Apparently, Popbottle Jones did the thinking and G. I. Jack did the head bobbing. "Last time Petunia ate a pair of socks, Doc fixed her right up. Didn't he, Popbottle?"

"Indeed he did."

Cheyenne wasn't about to ask about Petunia or her predilection for eating socks. Relieved to have a plan of action and eager to get on her way, she asked, "Where would I find this Dr. Bowman?"

Popbottle Jones pointed toward the east. "On the edge of town, about a half mile. Just follow Hope Avenue to Mercy Street."

It was all she could do not to roll her eyes. She puffed out a dry laugh. She was in a town called Redemption with virtuous street names like Hope and Mercy. Did these people actually believe that stuff?

As she climbed into her car, a tweak of conscience poked at her.

A long time ago, she'd believed in those things, too.

As the newcomer pulled away from the curb, Popbottle Jones rubbed his chin and watched her, knowingly. "Are you thinking what I'm thinking?"

G. I. Jack adjusted the bill of his cap, his focus also on the disappearing blue car. "Yep."

"Miss Cheyenne Rhodes is in trouble."

"Or runnin'."

"That's trouble, G.I."

"Yep. I've known soldiers like that. Walking wounded." He picked up a gunnysack of scavenged goods and hoisted the day's finds over one shoulder.

"My thoughts exactly." Popbottle Jones gave a wise nod and reached for his own sack. "Which means she's come to exactly the right place."

Chapter Two

Trace Bowman had never once regretted his decision to become a country veterinarian, but days like today stretched him to his limits. After a midnight house call to a local ranch, the clinic had been hopping with patients all day. Springtime brought puppies and calves and lambing ewes plus all manner of accidents, and as the only vet in town, he saw them all.

"Give her one of these morning and evening and bring her back to get the stitches out in about a week." He stroked the still drowsy cat who'd had an unfortunate run-in with the radiator fan of her owner's car. She was lucky to have come out with only a gash on her side.

"Thank you, Doctor. I'm sorry to keep you here so late. You look done in."

With a grin, he scraped a weary hand down his face and heard the scratch of unshaved beard. No doubt, he looked worse than his patients. After the midnight emergency at Herman Wagner's farm, he'd arrived at the clinic in time for the first surgery but not in time for morning ablutions. He'd done little more than scrub up and toss on a lab coat. He probably smelled worse than his patients, too. Without his mom to look after Zoey during those all-nighters, Trace didn't know what he would do.

"No problem, Mrs. James. That's what I'm here for. Call me if Precious needs anything else." His staff had left an hour ago, but that was typical. With his house located next to the clinic, he was frequently the one who left last and locked up.

After Mrs. James's departure, he made the rounds through the clinic, pausing to grin up at the lopsided sign hanging over the reception desk. Today is the Best Day Ever. He made a point to read the message morning and night as a reminder that each day was whatever he made of it. He'd learned that lesson the hard way. No matter how weary he was or how hectic the workload, he was a blessed man.

"Thanks, Lord," he murmured and continued his rounds.

Six dogs and three cats were spending the night, but none were critical enough to need his attention again until morning. Out in the dog-run four animals awaited adoption. He was normally successful in finding homes for the strays, mostly because he offered six months of free vet service. The way he looked at it, whatever worked. Euthanasia was not his favorite procedure.

Margo called him a sucker, but his seven-year-old daughter thought he was the biggest hero in America for taking in strays. He'd accept Zoey's opinion any day of the week, though Margo was a good woman. He liked her. They went to the same church and shared common interests, both being active in Redemption's civic groups. The trouble with Margo was that she'd started dropping hints lately about moving the relationship to another level, but Trace was not ready to go there. He wanted to be but he wasn't. Not yet anyway.

From the time Zoey's mother died, he'd prayed for the Lord to send the right woman into his life. His little girl needed a mother even more than he needed a wife. But so far, his heart refused to cooperate.

As he stuck his hands beneath the faucets and gave them one last warm, soapy scrub before heading home, he heard the front door scrape open. The noise was loud in the quiet, empty clinic, made louder by echoing concrete floors and a door that needed adjustment. A late patient, no doubt. With a sigh and a growling belly, he grabbed a paper towel and headed toward the front of the building.

A woman stood in the waiting room. Trace stopped dead in his tracks and stared, the bottom falling out of his stomach.

Hovering uncertainly in the dim, shadowy light was a young woman in faded jeans, T-shirt and fitted leather jacket. With flowing black hair and a fit, trim build, she looked enough like his late wife to make him dizzy.

He pressed a finger and thumb to eyes gritty from fatigue. On the second blink, the similarities faded. He was tired. That was all. The woman before him had the same build and coloring, but where Pamela's face was soft and ever smiling, this woman had a solemn-eyed toughness about her.

He tossed the towels at a trash can. "Can I help you?"

Her chin went up, her shoulders square as though she was ready to fight. Her gaze darted around the shadowy clinic before coming back to challenge him. His curiosity was piqued. Why did this pretty stranger need to be defensive? Had he done something he didn't know about?

"Are you the vet?" The question was almost an accusation. "Dr. Bowman?"

"That's me." Trace intentionally relaxed and

offered a smile to put the tightly wound woman at ease. "You must be new to Redemption. I don't think we've met before."

She thrust the box at him. "I found these stray pups on the side of the road."

Trace lifted an eyebrow. So much for small talk. He accepted the carton and placed it on the reception counter. Blame it on his state of exhaustion, but her attitude was not giving him much desire to cooperate.

"What do you want me to do with them?"

Some of the attitude went out of her. She floundered. "Well, I—Two old bums in town sent me. They said—I thought—"

Trace's sense of humor returned. "Popbottle Jones and G. I. Jack? They're not bums. Characters, yes. Bums, no."

"But they were Dumpster-diving."

His mouth curved. She wasn't the first to misjudge the two old dudes. "Don't say that to them. They call their vocation recycling, taking care of the environment, going green."

Her full bottom lip twitched and Trace felt an unexpected jolt of satisfaction. She'd be a knockout if she eased up and smiled more.

"Where I come from, Dumpster-diving is illegal."

Trace gave her his best smile, wanting inexplicably to warm up this frosty lady. "And where exactly do you come from?"

Any hint of friendless faded so fast Trace thought he'd imagined it. "What about the puppies? Can you take them?"

Trace reached into the box and withdrew a fat, wiggling body, trying to decide exactly why this woman intrigued him. It was pretty obvious she didn't like either men or vets or both. Or maybe she didn't like anyone at all. A little nudge on the inside told him to play nice. Like G. I. Jack and Popbottle Jones, there could be more to his visitor than met the eye.

"Why don't you keep them?"

As if annoyed even more by the question, the woman fisted her hands on her hips. "As you noticed, I'm new in town. I have nowhere to take them even if I were inclined to do so."

"And you aren't?"

"Not in the least."

"You don't like animals?"

"Everyone likes puppies."

Well, he felt better knowing that. "Where are you planning to stay?"

She took a step back as if the question was too personal. "I don't know yet. Will the puppies be all right here?"

He could see her genuine concern and again, he felt better. Trace prided himself on his ability to read people and he suspected Miss Hard-as-nails had a marshmallow interior she didn't want anyone to see. And that intrigued him more. What had happened to this pretty lady to make her so defensive?

"There's only one motel in town. Widow Wainright's place. Nothing fancy but clean and quiet and not too pricey. Tell her I sent you. Kitty will fix you up."

Dark eyes narrowed as if analyzing his motive. "Where would I find this place? If I was interested."

Oh, she was interested all right. Interested but cautious. The question was, why?

"Over on Charity Lane about five or six blocks off Main."

An incredulous expression crossed her face. "Charity Lane? Mercy Street. Hope Avenue. Redemption. What is this place? The twilight zone?"

Absently stroking the soft puppy, Trace laughed. "Nothing quite as exciting as that. According to town history, Redemption was founded during the Land Run of 1889 by a gunslinger turned preacher. He started Redemption for souls like him—people who wanted to change their ways and start fresh. The street names are his way of reminding us that everything we need is found in God's redeeming love."

His visitor stared at him with a troubled look and Trace thought for a minute he'd said too much. Margo claimed he sounded like a preacher at times and maybe he did. But as he studied the woman standing in his waiting room, he suspected something else. She'd reacted to the town names oddly because they were exactly why she was here. Like so many of the souls who arrived in Redemption, the tough cookie before him was in need.

"I'll take care of the puppies," he said softly.

Her stance relaxed the slightest bit. "Thanks."

"You can come visit them anytime."

"Oh, no, I—" She shrugged. "Maybe I will. Do you think you can find homes for them? I wouldn't want them to be—you know."

Hard shell on the outside, soft as puppy fur on the inside. "Puppies are pretty easy to re-home."

"Good." She gave a curt nod and turned as if to leave.

"Wait." He didn't know why but he wasn't ready for her to go.

She glanced over one shoulder before slowly pivoting, expression guarded.

"You didn't tell me your name."

She hesitated a second before saying, "Cheyenne Rhodes."

He offered his hand. "Well, Cheyenne Rhodes, welcome to Redemption. I hope you'll like our little town."

The guarded expression lingered as she slipped her hand into his. "I hope so, too."

Trace tried not to react to her skin against his, but her feminine hand was far softer than her expression and far more slender than his work-roughened one. "If I can help you with anything else—"

She pulled her hand away, cynicism firmly back in place. "Only if you know where I can find a job."

So Tough Girl was sticking around. Nice. "What kind of work do you do?"

Again, her hesitation piqued his curiosity.

"Anything for now."

"I can always use another hand here in the clinic." Which was true, though why he'd want to hire an unfriendly helper with a chip on her shoulder was more than he wanted to think about.

She shook her head. Loose black hair swished against the shiny maroon leather of her jacket. "I don't think so."

Was it the job that didn't suit her—or him? "Just a thought. I frequently hire temporaries to help out the full-time staffers. The clinic keeps us all busy."

"How many?"

"Employees?" At her nod, he said, "Three, right now. So what do you say? Pay's lousy, working conditions stink—literally—but the staff is friendly, the boss is a *great* guy, and you can play with the pups anytime."

She surprised him with a soft laugh. "Bribery."

He arched an eyebrow, teasing. "I'm a desperate man."

25

She tilted her head and studied him, a twinkle in her dark eyes. "Somehow I doubt that. You don't look the desperate type."

But he had been once, a truth that made it easy to recognize a fellow desperado.

He pointed a puppy at her. "Be here at nine in the morning and I'll put you to work. You can bring the doughnuts."

Dark eyebrows surged upward. "Doughnuts?"

"From the Sugar Shack."

"Let me guess," she said wryly. "It's located on Grace Boulevard."

Trace chuckled. The lady had a sense of humor. "No. Plain old Main Street at Town Square, next to the post office."

She thought about the offer so long Trace knew she was going to refuse. What he didn't expect was how disappointed he was when she did.

The drive to the motel on Charity Lane was short and easy and filled with thoughts of Trace Bowman, the friendly veterinarian.

"I should have taken that job," she muttered.

When she'd first walked into the empty, darkened building, being alone with a strange man had made her skin crawl. But even though he had been as scruffy looking as the two Dumpster-divers, the amiable vet had a way about him. When he'd teased her about doughnuts she'd almost said yes.

But she hadn't. He'd been too friendly, too accommodating, and her suspicion meter had gone off the charts. Nobody did something for nothing.

Though he wasn't overly large, he was taller than her by a head and far more muscular. Lean and fit with tanned arms strong enough to handle a large animal practice, he'd be a hard man to take down.

Still, she couldn't stop thinking about him. Beneath the unshaven face and mussed brown hair, he was undoubtedly attractive and not much older than herself, though most days she felt a hundred instead of thirty.

Attractive. Young. There was the problem. She found the kindhearted vet a bit too attractive, the exact kind of man she was inclined to fall for. The last thing she needed in her life was another man like Paul Ramos who would disappear the moment he learned about her late-night encounter with Dwight Hector.

Besides, he probably had women bringing in stray cats and dead birds and pet guppies as an excuse to see him. She didn't need that either.

She killed the car in front of a short row of maybe ten tidy cottages. The motel was old, likely built in the 50s or 60s, but well kept and pretty in a retro kind of way. The widow obviously liked plants because each unit came with a white window box of red geraniums, a short-clipped patch of grass in front and tidy shrubs growing close to the white siding. From the back of the establishment, huge oaks bent shady arms above each roof, letting in only dappled slices of sunshine. The effect was provincial, warm, peaceful. Cheyenne almost believed she would like it here.

Beneath a waving American flag, a sign outside said Redemption Motel and Gifts, Vacancy. Bible Study at 8.

Envisioning a gentle, white-haired widow who offered prayer and Proverbs with her tea, Cheyenne found her way to the unit marked Office and went inside. A bell above the door gave a merry jingle.

As she scanned the room in search of the proprietor, Cheyenne breathed in the smell of rose potpourri and cataloged the premises. The Widow Wainright was not only a Christian; she was a patriot who made extra money selling inspiration and Americana. The place was decorated in red, white and blue with American flags sprouting from potted plants, eagle-topped fountain pens crowded into coffee mugs and a display case filled with various other souvenirs and gift items. The walls were plastered with military photos and Uncle Sam posters. One of them pointed straight at her. Uncle Sam Wants You!

"Hello, hello. Sorry to keep you waiting." A tall, willowy blonde carrying a basket of snowy white towels swept into the office with an air of cheerfulness. Cheyenne did a double take. This young, beautiful woman could not be the Widow Wainright.

Pale hair pulled into a loose topknot with unfettered strands framing a delicate, heart-shaped face and wide blue eyes, she made Cheyenne think of a fairy-tale princess. There was a vulnerable sweetness about her completely out of context with Cheyenne's idea of an independent widow.

"Are you Mrs. Wainright?"

"Kitty, please. We don't stand on ceremony in Redemption."

So much for assumptions. "I'm Cheyenne Rhodes."

"How can I help you, Cheyenne? Need a room? Or just looking at the gift shop? I have some great gift ideas."

"A room please."

"You're in luck! I just happen to have a vacancy." She made a cute face and bunched slim shoulders in a girlish gesture. "Too many of them, actually, but that's the nature of Redemption. The only time I'm filled up is during the Land Run celebration." She dug out a registration form and pushed it across to Cheyenne. "New in town or passing through?"

Was everyone in this town nosy?

"New." Using one of the pens with a flying

eagle topper, Cheyenne bent her head to the form. "Do you have a room with cooking facilities?"

"Oh, sure. Half of my units are long-term rentals with kitchenettes. Otherwise, I couldn't keep the doors open." Kitty placed her forearms on the glass countertop. Rose potpourri stirred around her. Everything about this woman was fresh and clean and inviting. "Does this mean you'll be staying a while?"

"Until I find an apartment." Or move on.

"Great. You can come to our Bible study and meet some of the other townsfolk. Redemption is a nice place to settle."

As much as Cheyenne wanted to make friends and have a real life again, she wasn't excited about a Bible study. If she'd ever had any faith, it had disappeared the night Dwight Hector broke into her garage.

"If you'll just sign the guest register here." Kitty tapped a finger against the lined page. "I'll take down your credit card info and we'll be all set."

Feeling as if she'd stepped back in time, Cheyenne complied, waiting patiently while Kitty entered the numbers the old-fashioned way, without the use of a credit card machine. When the widow finished, she took Cheyenne's registration form to a metal file box.

"Well, look at that," she said, holding the card at an angle above the box. "You're from Colorado."

Cheyenne tensed; the thought raced through her head that Kitty had put the name and state together and come up with a news report.

"Formerly," she said, words terse and defensive.

Kitty lifted wistful blue eyes, apparently unaware of her guest's reaction. "My late husband and I honeymooned in the mountains near Breckenridge."

Cheyenne took a second to make the mental shift from her anxious thoughts to Kitty's meaning. The place steeped in pain and sorrow for Cheyenne was a place of loving memory for the young widow.

"The mountains are a beautiful honeymoon destination," she managed, wondering if she would ever stop feeling edgy and suspicious.

"Yes, they were." The woman stood for several seconds, lost in thought and probably in memories of the man she'd loved and lost. Cheyenne ached for her. Why did life have to be so cruel?

Not knowing what to say, she waited in an oddly comfortable silence. As a police officer, she'd done her share of bringing bad news to hapless families, but she'd never been around for the aftermath.

With a pat to her heart, Kitty's pink-glossed lips tilted, though her eyes remained sad. "I'll have to show you my photo album sometime."

"I'd like that. He must have been a great husband."

31

"The best." She fanned herself with Cheyenne's card. "I see Dr. Bowman recommended my fine establishment. You know Trace?"

"Not exactly." Cheyenne told the widow about the puppies.

"Well, that's Trace. He takes in all the strays. Always has."

Was that why he tried to hire her? Because she looked like a stray to be pitied? "So you've known him a long time?"

"Long enough to know he's a soft touch, but then everybody in Redemption knows everyone else. Familiarity is the blessing of small-town living."

Or maybe the curse.

"He offered me a job." Cheyenne added a light laugh as though the notion was facetious—and maybe it was. What kind of sensible human hired total strangers off the street without so much as a reference?

"Oooh." Kitty's eyes twinkled in speculation. "You must have made an impression."

Cheyenne stiffened, her guard firmly back in place. "He said he hires a lot of people."

Kitty laughed merrily. "Yes. He does. Trace is always trying to help someone and from what I've seen the clinic can use all the assistants he can find. I was teasing you, though you have to admit Trace Bowman is a cutie-pie."

"I didn't notice." Liar, liar.

Kitty laughed again. "Then you need to make an appointment with Dr. Spencer to have your eyes checked."

Cheyenne tweaked a shoulder. "Well, maybe I did notice."

Kitty slapped the top of the glass counter and set a half dozen military bobble-heads in motion. "Now you're talking. I may be a widow but I know *fine* when I see it. And that man is über-fine. Why didn't you take the job, you crazy woman?"

"Not the kind of work I'm looking for, but I do need a job, so if you know of anything . . ."

Kitty stuck a pencil through her blond top-knot. "What kind of job *do* you have in mind?"

Anything but the über-fine vet. "Office work, waitressing, retail, that kind of thing."

"Quite a variety there. I'll keep my ear to the ground. You'd do a lot better asking at the Sugar Shack, though. Everyone and everything filters through there. Talk to Miriam. She owns the place."

"All right. Thanks. I'll do that."

Kitty opened a drawer and took out a key. "This is for Unit 4. I'll walk over there with you to make sure the room suits you."

"I'm sure it's okay."

"Me, too, but I could use a little more girl talk." Blue eyes widened, she bunched her shoulders in a charming gesture. Kitty's delicate femininity

33

left Cheyenne feeling like a wrestler. "It's not every day I rent a room to someone near my age."

"All right, then, lead the way." As long as Kitty didn't pry too deeply, they could girl-talk all she wanted. Kitty could talk. Cheyenne would listen.

Exiting the office, they followed a curving graveled path past three motel doors, each bearing a shiny brass number. Red, white and blue impatiens bordered the gravel in a cheery repeat of Kitty's favorite color scheme.

"What brings you to Redemption, Cheyenne? Relatives?"

"I don't know a soul." And no one knows me. For the people of Redemption, she was a clean slate, just the way she wanted to be.

"No relatives and no job," Kitty said, "so that leaves only one other reason for coming here."

And Cheyenne hoped no one discovered what that reason was.

Knowing when to keep her mouth shut, she shoved her hands into her jacket pockets and stared down at the white gravel crunching beneath her boots.

Kitty raised a hand to greet someone. "Hi, Henry. Nice day for fishing. Going to the river?"

Cheyenne looked up. A middle-aged man, fishing rod over one shoulder, hoisted a tackle box in greeting.

"I sure am. Wanna come along?"

Kitty's merry laugh rang out. "Another time. Gotta wash your sheets today."

The man waved again and slammed the door of his truck. The engine roared, sending a puff of exhaust into the atmosphere as he pulled away.

Small-town friendliness was something Cheyenne would have to get used to.

Kitty picked up the conversation where she'd left off. "Redemption draws people, Cheyenne. I don't know how exactly but the Lord must lead them here."

A skeptical Cheyenne searched the motel owner's guileless face. Kitty Wainright seemed too nice to be one of those religious wackos. "You're saying God told me to come to this town?"

That was about as far from true as the woman could get.

"No." The sun gleamed off blond hair as Kitty shook her head. "I said He *leads* people—people who need what Redemption has to offer."

"I have to be honest with you, Kitty. I'm not sure what I believe about God anymore."

Kitty slid the room key into the door marked with the number 4. As she pushed it open and cool, potpourri-scented air wafted out, she turned and placed a hand on Cheyenne's arm. "Then I have good news for you, girl. Those with questions, those who are struggling, they're exactly the ones He leads to Redemption."

Chapter Three

Cheyenne awoke the next morning with a headache and the remnants of the dream lingering like a bad odor. She sat on the side of the bed, head in her hands, for several minutes to clear the fog.

Last night as usual, after checking and rechecking the locks, she'd lain awake for hours with the lights on. Her thoughts had run the gamut from the old bums to the handsome vet to Kitty's curious comment about God.

She'd stumbled onto the town of Redemption by accident. A spot on the map. A place to land. There was no other explanation. Certainly not some mystical voice from God.

She scrubbed at her face with both hands, ashamed of her cynical attitude. Kitty hadn't talked about voices, though her meaning was as mysterious as a voice would have been.

After a glance at the clock-radio, Cheyenne dragged herself out of bed and to the shower. Today was the first day of the rest of her life and she was determined to find a job and get on with living.

By the time she was dressed and ready to hunt down the Sugar Shack, her cell phone jingled. After checking the caller ID, she answered. "Hi, Brent."

"Hey, sis." Her brother's deep voice eased an ache in her chest. "Where are you? Still sleeping in your car?"

"Believe it or not, no." She looked around the motel room. Kitty took pains to make the units more homey than most. "I'm in a motel in Redemption, a little town in Oklahoma."

Brent whistled. "Long way from home, sis."

"Which is what we all agreed was best."

"I know. Still—"

"A fresh start, new faces and time to forget."

"You can come home anytime, Chey. Dad and I will take care of you."

She wanted to take care of herself again, not huddle in her bedroom afraid of shadows and cruel speculation. Her dad and brother thought she should "put what happened behind her," to "forget about it" and move on. She knew they meant well and she longed to follow their advice. She simply had not been able to do so.

"Maybe someday when things blow over."

She reached under the pillow and moved a gun to her purse. Kitty probably wouldn't appreciate knowing her new renter slept with a nine-millimeter Glock. Though Cheyenne never wanted to use the weapon again, she couldn't fall asleep without that lethal assurance. Even then, sleep was fitful and filled with things she didn't want to remember.

"You should see this place, Brent. Redemption is like a step back in time. Homey, friendly." She told him about the Dumpster-divers and savored his warm laugh. "They were interesting, let me tell you."

"I can imagine," he said dryly.

"And the woman who owns the motel hosts a Bible study every night."

Cynic that he was, Cheyenne could imagine Brent's grimace. "Look out for weirdos."

"She's not like that. Really. Although she said something strange about God leading needy souls to Redemption. Or some such."

"Told you. Weirdo."

Cheyenne pushed a strand of hair back from her forehead and grinned. "You always know how to cheer me up."

"You're not planning to stay there in Weirdo-ville, are you?"

"For now. I'm job-hunting today."

"Where?"

She heard the tension in his tone.

"Not police work." Heaviness pulled on her insides like lead weights. "I know I can't do that anymore, Brent."

"I'm sorry, sis," he said softly.

"Me, too." More than sorry, she was brokenhearted. Being a police officer had been her life's ambition.

"How are you otherwise?"

She knew what he meant. They never discussed the incident that had changed her life. Like everyone else, Brent and her father had wanted to pretend nothing had happened to her. If they didn't talk about it, the issue would go away. They were wrong.

The silence of friends and coworkers was one of the reasons she'd left Colorado Springs. No one but the antagonistic press wanted to discuss that night. No one wanted to admit that something terrible and life-changing had happened to strong, sensible Detective Rhodes. She looked all right on the outside, so she must be fine. Only she knew how wrong they were.

The news media reminded her on a regular basis. Even after the investigation and the grand jury, reporters and gun-law activists stayed in her face. They were the second reason she'd fled her hometown.

The other reasons went deeper and she suspected they'd followed her here.

"I'm coping." She would never be the same and she would always wonder what she'd done to deserve such a thing happening to her, but she was determined to keep living. Dwight Hector had hurt her. He'd stolen her peace, her sense of security, her relationships, her career and a year of her life, but she would not let him destroy her.

"Good. Good." He paused before continuing. "I guess you haven't heard the latest news."

"Good or bad?"

"Depends on your perspective, I guess. But it's news I didn't want you to hear from someone else."

"Am I being prosecuted?"

"Chey, no. That's over. You were cleared of all wrongdoing."

After her being under a cloud of suspicion for a year, the final ruling still didn't register.

"I keep expecting something else to pop up." Like Dwight Hector, though she'd watched him die and knew he would never hurt another woman. She pushed at her hair and sighed. "I don't know. I'm so tired of it all."

"Let the past go, sis. Be healed and happy again. I miss you." Her brother's pensive voice wrapped around her with love.

"So what's the big news?"

A moment of silence told her she wasn't going to like his message.

Brent cleared his throat.

"Spit it out, Brent. I'm immune to bad news."

"Right. That's why you're in some hick town called Redemption."

"Redemption is not a hick town. I like—" She stopped the sentence, realizing Brent was stalling. *"Tell me."*

"Paul is getting married. To Melinda."

Her eyes fell shut as she imagined her former fiancé marrying someone else, a someone else who happened to be her friend. "Good for them. I'll send a card."

"Are you okay?"

"Never better."

"I'm sorry."

"Forget it, Brent. Paul walked out on me when I needed him most. Why would I care about a man like that?"

"Right. Okay. Sure."

She'd adored Paul Ramos, but now she felt nothing but sadness—not for Paul, but for the woman she'd become. A woman no man would want. Paul had taught her that.

A lull ensued when neither could think of anything to say and Cheyenne ended the call. She loved her only two relatives, but they had been adversely affected, too. Whether they admitted it or not, and no matter how much she hurt to know, Dad and Brent were glad to have her gone.

The Sugar Shack smelled sweet enough to give her a toothache. If the crowd gathered at round tables and along a low counter with stools was any indication, the Sugar Shack was the local meeting place, at least for breakfast. Besides the scrumptious pastries and breads filling the dis-

41

play cases and tinting the air with a warm, yeasty fragrance, the shop served country breakfast fare and sandwiches.

As she stood inside the door, analyzing the inhabitants, several heads turned her direction. But instead of suspicion, their expressions showed only momentary interest before they turned back to their companions or their steaming coffee cups. After looking for a seat and finding none, Cheyenne made her way toward the cash register. The chatter of friendly voices mingled with the clink of thick white mugs against matching saucers and the occasional *ka-ching* of the cash register. A few customers nodded a polite greeting as she walked by.

The small gesture buoyed her.

As she turned sideways to ease around one table, a voice called out, "Miss Cheyenne."

She glanced down into the whiskery face of G. I. Jack.

"Did Doc Bowman take the puppies?"

The grizzled old bum had an undeniable sweetness about him. She smiled. "He did."

The man pushed at the extra chair between himself and Popbottle Jones. "You'll not find another empty. Sit down and we'll treat you to breakfast. Won't we, Popbottle?"

His Dumpster partner hoisted a cup in her honor. "Indeed we will."

They'd treat her? These two raggedy old

derelicts? "Oh, I couldn't, but I will share your table if you don't mind."

G. I. Jack frowned, thick bushy eyebrows pulled together in bewilderment. "Why would we mind? We invited you."

Barely holding back a grin, Cheyenne took the offered chair. "This place is busy."

"Always is. Best biscuits and gravy you'll find anywhere." He poked a forkful of the afore-mentioned food into his mouth.

"Thank you for your help yesterday."

"Glad to be of assistance."

"Good because I'd like to ask you something else." Considering how full his mouth was, she didn't wait for his reply. "I need a job. Any kind of job."

G. I. Jack's brow creased in thought, but he kept right on shoveling food into his mouth.

Popbottle Jones lowered his coffee cup. "Dr. Bowman hires a person now and then."

The handsome vet again.

A stick-thin woman in a baker's apron sashayed up to the table. Graying black hair yanked straight back from an angular face met in a bun at the nape of her neck. Long, bony hands with overlarge knuckles wielded a pad and pen.

Cheyenne gave her order before saying, "I'd like to speak with Miriam. Is she here?"

"She sure is."

G. I. Jack and Popbottle Jones chuckled. The

woman shook her pencil at them before turning a friendly look to Cheyenne. "I'm Miriam. Whatcha need?"

Popbottle Jones laid aside his fork. "She's new in town. Her name is Cheyenne."

"She's looking for a job." Without the least bit of self-consciousness, G. I. Jack slid a fluffy biscuit into his shirt pocket. Yesterday fries, today biscuits. "She's staying over to Kitty's. And she likes dogs."

How did they know where she was staying?

"Well, let's see." Miriam took the order pad, ripped off a page, turned the sheet over and began to write. When she finished, she handed the short list to Cheyenne. "A lot of places have shut down in the past few months or cut back. The economy, you know. But these are worth a shot."

"I appreciate your help." As Cheyenne started to fold the list, Miriam reached for the paper again.

"Wait. I thought of one more place. G.I. said you like dogs."

Cheyenne had a feeling she knew what Miriam was writing. Sure enough, when she took the paper, there he was again—Trace Bowman.

By noon, she'd gone through the list of potential employers and found nothing but a town filled with mostly friendly folks and an assortment of entertaining characters. Worse, she kept hearing about the bad economy and Trace Bowman.

"Is there some kind of conspiracy in this town to find the vet an assistant?" she muttered as she slid behind the wheel of her car and slammed the door, discouraged.

Just as she cranked the engine, her cell phone jingled.

Cheyenne's eyebrows lifted. Brent again? She punched Talk. "Is something wrong?"

"Nah, just wanted to hear your voice."

"Right. Two calls in one day means something. What's up?"

"No hurry, but if you're settling in Weirdo-ville for a while, I'll forward your mail. You've got some bills here."

"Lovely. More bills. I thought I had everything paid. What are they?"

She heard the swish of paper as he shifted through the envelopes and rattled off a few minor debts. "Anything major?"

"Law offices of Windom and Green . . ."

Cheyenne groaned. She'd already paid them an enormous amount. "How much is that one?"

"I'll have to open it."

"Go ahead."

She heard the rip and then the hiss of indrawn breath.

"Wow." He named a sum that made her gasp as well. Her remaining severance pay from the police department wouldn't cover the amount. The price of proving oneself guilty of nothing except being a madman's victim was exorbitant.

After giving Brent the address of the motel and assuring him she had everything under control, she flipped the cell phone shut and leaned her head on the steering wheel. On the floorboard lay Miriam Martinelli's job list. With a sigh of resignation, she picked up the paper. All but one suggestion was crossed off.

Dr. Trace Bowman.

"Dr. Bowman, Barry is on the phone. His raccoon has diarrhea." Jeri Burdine, the middle-aged assistant who answered the phones and maintained the clinic accounts, peered around the doorway of Exam Room One. Bright beads rattled at the ends of tidy black cornrows.

Trace barely looked up from examining a dog with a high fever.

"Tell Barry the treatment's the same as usual. Give him a teaspoon of Kaopectate every four hours as needed. No food, but a lot of liquids, especially Gatorade. Bring him in if he's not better tomorrow." Ten-year-old Barry was a kid after his own heart. He rescued critters, the latest being a baby raccoon whose mother had been hit by a car.

The coffee-brown face flashed a grin. "Will do."

A cacophony of yapping dogs had Trace raising his voice to be heard. "And tell Toby to check that sheltie pup in the kennel again. I have a bad feeling."

"Got it." Jeri's wide hips sashayed away with her usual cheerful efficiency. Some days he wished for a dozen Jeris. Days like today.

One hand around a slim muzzle, Trace slid a needle into the dachshund on the table. The clinic was busier today than yesterday. Every member of his staff was moving as quickly as possible but the line in the waiting room grew longer. His thoughts flashed to Cheyenne Rhodes, the woman he'd tried to hire last night. Too bad she'd turned him down. He would have hired three of her, bad attitude and all.

Gently, he opened the dog's mouth and shone a flashlight inside for the owner to see. "She has a bad tooth that needs to come out but not until the infection resolves. This shot will get her started but you'll need to give her some pills at home."

"So that's why she won't eat."

"Would you?"

The teen shuddered. "No way. Poor baby."

Once Trace was finished, the teen gathered the dog into her arms and left. As he walked her down the hallway to the reception desk, Cheyenne Rhodes came striding through the entrance. As had happened last night, his heart jump-started. The bristly woman had a strange effect on his cardiac muscle.

"Afternoon," he said, suddenly not as busy as he thought he was. "Here to see the puppies?"

"Not really." She tossed her hair back in a self-conscious gesture. "I mean, I'd like to, but that's not why I'm here."

"No?" Trace felt a bewildering zing of energy. "All right, then. Come on back. We'll talk while you say hello to the pups. They'll like that."

He led the way down the hall, past a room in which his bubbly red-haired assistant, Jilly Fairmont, was grooming a poodle, and made a left turn toward the kennel area. "I hope you don't mind the smell of bleach. We disinfect the pens and floors a couple of times a day."

"Smells clean to me."

Her acceptance pleased him. Some women, specifically Margo, curled her nose and avoided the kennel as much as possible. He should have understood, but her reaction had always hurt his feelings.

"Here they are. Frog and Toad. My daughter named them after her favorite book characters." He squatted before the wire kennel and clicked up the latch. Zoey named all the animals, no matter how brief their stay. "Hey, little dudes. Look who came to see you."

His shoes scraped the concrete as he pivoted toward Cheyenne. She crouched down as well, bringing her lean, jean-clad form close to his. He was a Christian but he was also a man, and it was difficult not to notice how pretty she looked in snug jeans and fitted top.

Handing her one of the pups, he kept the other, and watched as Cheyenne raised the animal to her cheek and closed her eyes. The pup rewarded her kindness with a few licks.

Jilly poked her head into the kennel. Rust-colored freckles stood out against pale white skin. "Doctor, we're ready in the surgery suite when you are."

"Be right there." He glanced at his visitor. "Sorry, I have to get back to work. You can stay with the puppies as long as you like."

She rose with him, still cradling the small dog. "Before you go—about that job you offered last night . . ."

He stopped in his tracks, surprised but hoping. "Are you asking if the offer still stands?"

She bit down on her lip before saying a reluctant "Yes."

Trace studied the darkly pretty woman before him. She didn't want to take the job, but she was going to. He probably should resent her attitude, but he was just glad she'd come back. He suspected that Cheyenne needed the job for more reasons than a paycheck. Maybe the Lord had sent her. Maybe she needed the warm, accepting love of cats and dogs.

And he could use the help. Maybe he also wanted to know her better. For ministry purposes of course. And if he was a little too happy about the prospect of getting to know Cheyenne Rhodes, so be it.

Chapter Four

Within minutes, Cheyenne had shucked her leather jacket to follow Dr. Bowman around the clinic, observing and learning.

"No time for formal training," Trace said. "If you see something that needs doing, ask someone or just do it."

He handed her a five-by-seven index card, listing info for Bennie, a fat beagle with skin allergies. "We make notes on these. Rabies inoculation updates, worming, anything pertinent that will go into the permanent chart later. I'll tell you as we work."

She hadn't expected to start immediately and she certainly hadn't expected to assist the man himself. But she took the card and read the entries already on it.

"He's been a patient since he was a pup," she

murmured, half to herself. "You must be a good doctor to inspire such loyalty."

"Not necessarily." Trace flashed a sparkly grin. "I'm the only vet for fifty miles. It's me or nothing."

Good-looking and self-effacing, too. Why couldn't he be more of a jerk so she could dislike him for a reason other than his Y chromosome?

"Are you?"

"What?" With one hand resting on the dog's back and the other rubbing the animal's long ears, he glanced up. "A good vet?"

She nodded, looking away from a gorgeous pair of light blue eyes. Yesterday, she'd been in such a state she'd barely noticed. Now she did, just as she noticed the slight indention in his left cheek and the faint lines of fatigue around his eyes and mouth. She also noticed that his left hand was ringless. Hadn't he mentioned a daughter? She'd feel a lot more comfortable if he was married with a dozen kids. Although a wife was no real indicator of what a man was or wasn't capable of.

"I do what I can."

"Don't let his modesty fool you. He's the best," offered the beagle's owner, a thirtysomething woman in a blue nurse's smock and sensible white shoes.

"I could return the compliment." To Cheyenne

51

he said, "You probably haven't met Annie Markham. Annie, this is Cheyenne Rhodes. She's new in town."

The women exchanged pleasantries before Trace went on, "Annie is a home health care nurse. The older folks of Redemption have nominated her for sainthood."

Annie laughed. "Oh, right. Tell that to Ted Sikes. He threatened to shoot me off the porch if I drew another vial of blood."

Despite the fatigue around her green eyes, Annie Markham was an attractive woman. Honey-blond bangs and hair pulled back in a ponytail framed a face with clear, translucent skin. As far as Cheyenne could tell, she wore no makeup and yet her eyes were rimmed with dark lashes. With a strange twinge, she wondered if Trace was interested in Annie Markham.

"Ted threatens everyone," Trace said, eyes twinkling. "I heard he told the mailman not to deliver another piece of junk mail or he was toast."

"That sounds like Ted, the silly old goose."

Trace looked at Cheyenne and pointed toward the corner. "Hand me the big white bottle on the second shelf."

Bottles and boxes, glass-fronted cabinets and interesting tools lined the walls and cluttered the countertops. Cheyenne went to the cabinet he indicated.

"This?" she asked, rattling pills as she lifted a bottle toward him.

"That's the one." He took the medication and counted out thirty tablets, then scribbled something on a small blue packet before sliding the pills inside.

"Is this Ted guy dangerous?" Cheyenne asked, her cop instinct kicking in.

Trace pried open the beagle's mouth, popped a pill inside and then gently rubbed the animal's throat. "Old Ted likes to bluster, but I don't think he'd hurt anyone, do you, Annie?"

"Ted? No. You should see him when I have the kids with me. Gives them candy, lets them have races on his treadmill and gather eggs from the chicken coop. They scare the chickens half to death, but Ted just cackles like the hens."

So Annie was married with children. Not that Cheyenne cared one way or the other.

"Speaking of the kids. How are they doing?" Trace asked.

"Looking forward to summer break."

"Zoey, too."

"Summer's great for kids. Not so great for single moms."

"Or dads," Trace said.

Okay, so they were both single. And attractive. Big whoop. She wasn't here to admire the vet. She was here to work.

"They'll be relieved to know their beloved

53

Bennie will be all right," Annie was saying.

At the mention of his name, the beagle looked up with sad eyes and moaned. All three adults laughed.

"Bennie needs to lose a few pounds and stay out of the tall grass and weeds. These allergy capsules, one each day, should suppress the worst of the skin rash. You know the drill. Other than that, Bennie is as good as new." Dr. Bowman handed Annie the small blue package. "Tell the kids to come over this summer and swim with Zoey."

"They'd love that. Thanks, Doc."

Trace set Bennie on the floor and snapped a thin cloth leash into the ring on his collar. He handed the end to Annie. "Are you still looking after Miss Lydia?"

"Every day."

"How's she doing?"

Annie paused, a sad look crossing her face. "You know Lydia. If you ask her, she'll smile that sweet smile, tell you she's dandy and then ask about you. By the time the conversation is over, *I* feel better but I haven't helped her much."

"How bad is she?"

"Her heart gets weaker all the time. And lately, she's really slowed down. Winter was hard on her. She hasn't spent one day this spring in her flowers." Annie started toward the door. "You know how beautiful her flowers always are."

Trace politely reached around and opened the exam-room door. "I'm sorry to hear that. Tell her she's in my prayers."

"I will."

Cheyenne listened in as Trace and Annie Markham stood in the hallway and chatted a while longer about the Lydia woman with the pretty flowers and great attitude. She felt like an outsider, which she was, but she appreciated the way both Trace and the nurse glanced her way, including her in the conversation, even though she had nothing to add.

After a bit, with Bennie moping along beside her, Annie said her goodbyes and left.

"She seems nice," Cheyenne said as she and the vet walked down the narrow hallway to the reception area.

"Annie? Yeah. She's had a rough few years but she's stayed strong."

Cheyenne didn't know whether to ask for details or remain quiet. She chose the latter.

"Dr. Bowman?"

Trace turned toward the voice. Jilly, his other assistant, stood in the door leading to the kennels. "Do you have a minute to help me with this horse?"

"Be right there." He handed Cheyenne Bennie's manila folder. "Would you give this to Jeri at the desk?"

"Sure." She took the chart to the reception area.

A middle-aged woman with dozens of neat, tiny braids covering her head and forty extra pounds, mostly on her hips, manned the desk. From what Cheyenne had observed in the short time she'd been there, Jeri Burdine was as grossly overworked as her boss. She booked appointments, escorted patients, answered the phone and collected payments, stocked shelves and generally ran the business end of the clinic.

"If you'll show me what you want done, I'll help," she told Jeri. "I don't think the doctor needs me right now."

Jeri pushed at a pair of rectangular reading glasses. "Girl, you don't have to ask twice. We have billing to do. Get your cute self back here and I'll show you. There's nothing to it but good record keeping."

With an inward grin at the woman's friendly chatter, Cheyenne said, "I can handle that."

A cop kept good records or paid the price in court.

In minutes she was sliding bills into envelopes and slapping on computer-generated mailing labels. Some of the bills were seriously overdue. "Does he charge a late fee?"

"A what?" Jeri looked at her curiously. "Dr. Bowman? You gotta be kidding."

Well, no, she wouldn't kid about a thing like that. This was a business, not a charity. But she kept her opinion to herself.

She was piling a stack of envelopes into an outgoing mail container when the outside door burst open. Instinctively, Cheyenne jerked toward the sound, hand going to her nonexistent revolver. A woman's frantic voice raised the hair on her arms.

"My puppy is hurt bad. Can you help?" The voice quivered as she held out the limp body of a very small Yorkshire terrier.

Cheyenne dropped the pile of envelopes and moved into action. "What happened?"

The young woman cast a furtive glance behind her. "Uh, he—uh, my husband stepped on him by accident. He didn't mean to. Chauncy got underfoot and he's so little. Ray would never hurt him on purpose."

Some instinct warned Cheyenne that the woman was being less than truthful. She protested just a little too much. About that time, a hulking man came through the door. His focus went immediately toward the shaking woman.

"Emma." The tone, instead of tender and concerned, was harsh.

The woman jumped, her eyes widened in fear. "They're getting the doctor now, Ray."

Her look pleaded with Cheyenne to agree.

Something was not right here. Every cop instinct inside her was screaming.

Jeri took one look at the injured animal and said to Cheyenne, "Take them on back to the exam room. I'll get Dr. Bowman."

As a cop Cheyenne had worked accidents, murders, shootings and just about every violent crime known to man. She'd seen unspeakable injuries up close and personal. Open wounds didn't shake her. But the dog was basically a ball of bloody fur. Even the smell was deathly.

The woman named Emma was trembling like an earthquake. "Is he going to die?"

Probably. But Cheyenne didn't say that.

"Quit bawling, Emma," the man said. "If he dies I'll get you another one."

Yeah, as if that was going to help. Cheyenne wanted to clobber the insensitive clod.

Instead she asked, "Is your dog a regular patient of Dr. Bowman's?"

"No." Tears raced down Emma's face and dripped on the dog. She was crying but doing her best not to make a sound. The effort worried Cheyenne. This was a traumatic event. Why should her husband be angry if she cried?

"No problem. What's his name?"

"Chauncey Ray. He's named after my husband."

"I bought him as a special gift for her birthday. Didn't I, Emma?"

Cheyenne managed a smile. She'd never had time for an animal and couldn't comprehend the attachment pet owners felt for their furry friends. But she understood heartache.

The man placed a hand on Emma's shoulder. She tensed.

Cheyenne narrowed her eyes in thought. There was a smugness about this Ray character that set her nerves on edge. She couldn't put her finger on the problem, but her cop gut labeled him a jerk.

They met Dr. Bowman in the hallway. "What's the emergency?"

Emma's waterworks restarted. She shook all over, far more than the situation warranted. Her husband gave her an annoyed look and said, "The dumb dog got underfoot." He lifted a heavy boot, almost grinning as if he was proud. "I got a pretty big foot. I told her to keep him out of the way."

Trace gave the man a cool glance. "Put him on the table, and let me have a look."

The woman did as she was told, small hands trembling as she gently laid the tiny dog on the paper-covered table.

Cheyenne saw then what she'd missed in the hallway. Bruises on the inside of Emma's upper arms. Fingerprint bruises. She looked closer. The faint outline of a handprint marred the woman's cheek. Earlier, Cheyenne had dismissed the red cheek as the result of crying. Now she had a different thought.

Her hackles rose. This oversize clod was hitting his wife. And she wouldn't be a bit surprised if he'd hurt the dog intentionally.

"Is he going to die?" Emma asked again, standing back from the exam table. Her husband put an arm around her, but she did not look comforted.

"Let's get some pain medication into him first and then we can do some X-rays to see what kind of damage we're dealing with." Dr. Bowman offered Emma an encouraging glance, before turning his full attention on the dog. "Think positive. Injuries are not always as bad they initially appear."

Cheyenne, cynic that she was, figured he said that to everyone. She'd already pegged him for a male Pollyanna.

He reached behind her for a bottle and syringe. Cheyenne dipped a shoulder, uncomfortable when his forearm brushed against her.

"You'll have to assist," he said, plunging a needle into a rubber stopper. "Jilly's busy with that mare's feet."

Cheyenne's stomach lurched. Assist with what? She was accustomed to investigating the aftermath. Accidents never happened when a police officer was watching.

An unpleasant emptiness spread through her. She wasn't a police officer anymore. What she had or had not done before did not apply in this scenario. She was a veterinary assistant now. She clamped down on her back molars.

Deal with it, Rhodes.

Keeping her expression bland, she muttered, "Sure. Whatever."

"Ma'am, would you and your husband prefer to wait in the waiting area?"

Emma's lips quivered. "Whatever you think is best."

Her husband gripped her arm. "You heard what he said. Come on."

With one jerky nod, Emma pivoted and left the room with her husband.

Expression grim, Trace glanced toward the door. "What's wrong with that picture?"

"I was thinking the same thing. Do you think he hurt this dog on purpose?"

"I wouldn't be surprised."

"He abuses her."

Trace glanced up, surprised. "How do you know that?"

"Observance. She has bruises on her arms and a handprint on her cheek. They'd been fighting when this happened."

"All the more reason to think he stomped or kicked this little dog. The injuries are not consistent with merely being stepped on."

"Can you save him?"

"Gotta try." His intelligent eyes studied the unmoving animal. "We'll have a better idea after the X-rays and a thorough exam. You up for this?"

Cheyenne gave one short nod. She'd handled plenty worse.

Over the next few minutes, the vet instructed her in restraining and positioning the limp little animal while he ran an X-ray machine. All the while, her mind whirled with the ramifications of the couple in the waiting room. A woman shouldn't put up with a man like that.

"Wear this." Trace tossed her an apron that weighed a ton.

"What's in this thing? Bricks?" She draped the gray apron around her neck.

"Close. Lead. Keeps you from being exposed to radiation." He disappeared behind a short wall. The hum and thump of the machine filled the room. Trace reappeared to reposition the animal again. "A couple more."

Cheyenne kept her hands where he instructed while he finished the procedure.

"All done. Hang the apron inside here and then stay with Chauncey while I process these."

He disappeared again and Cheyenne stared down at the sedated dog. He was a mess. Blood coated his golden brown coat. Cheyenne was pretty sure the white protrusion on his leg was a bone.

She shivered and tried to think of something else.

Noises came from behind her. Thumps and thuds. Buzzes and bells. And then the vet was back again, standing next to her. His focus was on the patient, but Cheyenne edged away from him and the peculiar sizzle of nerve endings he caused. She didn't know whether she liked or hated the feeling, but liking it wasn't an option.

"Other than the mangled leg, I don't see anything life-threatening."

She flicked him a glance. "Seriously?"

"I'll need to keep him overnight to rule out internal injuries, but he doesn't seem to be as bad as I first thought. I wasn't kidding when I said sometimes the worst-looking injuries end up not being so bad after all."

"That's true. I've seen people I didn't think would survive but they did."

He swiveled toward her, expression curious. "You have?"

Cheyenne mentally kicked herself. She hadn't intended to discuss her former life with anyone in Redemption. Let the past lie buried. If it would.

Avoiding the doctor's intensely blue eyes, she fiddled with the crinkly paper beneath the Yorkie. "I just meant—you know, on the road and stuff."

Dr. Bowman didn't respond, but she could feel him looking at her, curious. At least she thought she could. Lately, her emotions didn't always line up with reality. She knew this but she couldn't always control it.

Lack of control made her mad. Life in general made her mad. The feelings thrashing and banging around inside every time Trace Bowman came close made her mad.

But then, she'd been mad for the past year. Had she really expected things to improve just because a town was called Redemption?

Trace shook droplets of water from his hands and reached for a paper towel. The surgery on the Yorkie's leg had taken longer than he'd hoped, so Jeri had sent waiting patients home until tomorrow. A half dozen of the sickest had chosen to wait, but the injured dog was resting peacefully, still sedated, in a soft enclosure.

The pet owners had left, although the man had been blunt about not running up a huge vet bill. "Put him to sleep. I'll get her another."

Trace usually liked everyone. He couldn't say that about this guy. "That won't be necessary. We can work something out."

"I'll hold you to that, Doc." And with that warning he had ushered his wife from the clinic.

Some people.

With a weary sigh, he shot a look at his new assistant. She was an enigma. Not very friendly, either, but he'd known that when he hired her.

Even though the capable Jilly had returned, once the surgery was set up and ready he'd called Cheyenne in to help, too. Some perverse part of him must admire a tough woman with a chip on her shoulder.

Troubled. He could see it in the tense set of her shoulders and jaw. He could hear it in her terse answers. And he could read it in her soulful glares and the way she overprotected her three feet of personal space.

The question was why? And what exactly did the Lord expect him to do about Cheyenne Rhodes?

"Pretty good assistant for a first timer." In a light tone, Trace tossed the compliment casually over his shoulder but didn't move in her direction. He'd already discovered that if he got too close, her defenses went up and she'd back away. "You didn't faint or gag or run away."

"I don't faint." She stated the fact as though slightly insulted. He noticed she didn't mention the other two.

"You'd be surprised how many grown men turn pale when I start drilling into bone."

She shrugged one shoulder. "You did the hard part. All I did was play gofer."

He turned slowly, leaning his hips on the sink behind him as he dried his hands. "Appropriate job in an animal hospital, don't you think? A gopher."

Her full lower lip curved. "Have you ever treated a gopher?"

Trace felt a rush of energy through his very

tired body. Any hint that he was getting through that iron wall of hers cheered him immensely.

"This is a community of tulips and smooth, green lawns. Saving a gopher could get me tarred, feathered and run out of town."

For a nanosecond her dark, dark eyes twinkled and he held out the hope that she'd come back with a snappy retort. She turned her back instead. Stainless steel surgical tools clattered against a metal basin as she dunked them into antiseptic cleaning liquid. "What do I do with these after they're washed?"

Fighting down a frisson of disappointment, Trace studied his new employee's stiff shoulders. Did friendly conversation always make her nervous?

Lord, I'm trying, so give me a little direction here, okay?

"Toss them in that box for a trip to the autoclave." He ripped a couple more paper towels from the dispenser and sprayed antiseptic cleaner on the metal table. "I can't stop thinking about that couple."

The comment forced her to look back over one tense shoulder. "Me, too."

"Think we should contact the police?"

"Won't do any good."

"How do you know that?"

She hesitated for one brief second before turning back to the sink. "I just know."

Spoken like a woman with secrets.

He threw the paper towels in the trash can and studied his assistant. For the first day of work, she'd done all right. But her work ethic wasn't what concerned him. The way he felt with her in the room did.

She was puzzling and bristly. Yet despite those negatives, he wanted to know her better.

Her hair pooled like black ink against the blue lab jacket he'd loaned her. There was something about Cheyenne Rhodes that made him want to go on looking at her. He felt a little stupid about that. The woman was pretty, sure, but so was Margo, and though they'd dated off and on for a year, he'd never wanted to stand and stare at Margo Starks. Cheyenne's beauty wasn't the thing that intrigued him, really. Rather, he was fascinated by the way she narrowed her eyes in speculation, the way she held herself aloof and the subtle sense he had that she was hurting every single minute.

Something was sorely wrong in Cheyenne's world, and he was a doctor, a man called and trained to ease suffering. He wouldn't rest until her wounds, whatever they might be, were healed.

Chapter Five

Cheyenne was feeling better about her new job. Maybe this would work out all right after all. The vet was easygoing and didn't lose patience even when she couldn't find something. The other women were cordial, even though the clinic buzzed with patients, phone calls and animal sounds until they seldom had a spare moment. Cheyenne figured this was a good thing. Being busy kept her mind off everything else. Everything, that is, except the handsome vet. All he had to do was walk into the room and a buzz of energy shimmied along her nerve endings.

After feeling dead inside for so long, the reawakening stung like frozen fingers warmed too quickly. Wisdom warned to tread carefully.

Last night, when she'd arrived at the motel, her thoughts were torn between the too-attractive vet and the Yorkie owner. She was convinced Emma was a battered wife. This morning the husband had picked up the dog, paid the bill and left without a thank-you.

Cheyenne couldn't help wondering where Emma was. But she'd dealt with plenty of abuse victims and as long as they lied for their abusers, there was nothing anyone could do.

The knowledge burned inside her. She hated feeling impotent.

Over the spray of water, Cheyenne caught the sound of a humming baritone. At the moment, Dr. Bowman was at the sink, scrubbing up after the suture of a lacerated ferret. The vet was a happy guy. Either that or he put on a good act.

"Doc? You in here?"

The voice was male, but the words were thick and carefully formed as though the speaker had a speech impediment.

Curious, Cheyenne dumped the washed instruments into a box marked Redemption River Animal Clinic, threw a wad of empty plastic packaging into the trash and turned toward the opened door. A young man, probably in his late teens, with the rounded body and moon face of Down's syndrome shuffled into the room.

When he spotted Cheyenne, he stopped. Face a mix of confusion, curiosity and friendliness, he blinked rapidly. "Hello. I don't know you."

The air stirred and her skin prickled with awareness, a sure sign the singing vet had moved into her radar range. Annoyed to be so vulnerable, she took a step to one side.

"Toby," Trace said. "Come in and meet our new helper, Cheyenne."

Expression sweet and friendly, the teen stuck out his hand. "Hi."

Cheyenne took the spongy fingers in hers and shook. "Hello, Toby. I'm glad to know you."

"Toby is my right-hand man," Trace went on. "He keeps the kennels and cages in tip-top shape, feeds and waters and exercises. Couldn't run the place without him."

Toby responded with a huge grin. "Dr. Bowman likes me. I'm a good worker."

"I didn't see you on my first day. Were you here?"

"Wednesdays I'm not here. I got appointments. Doc cleans up for me. But the rest of the time, Toby does it." He patted his chest with the flat of one hand.

Though wearing a man's body, Toby was child-like and likeable and touched a soft spot in her heart. "I noticed how clean the kennels are."

"Yeah. Doc showed me how to make them really, really clean. Only put one little bitty cup of bleach in the bucket. Right, Doc?"

"Right, and no one does a better job than you."

"Not even you?"

"Not even me." Trace clapped the boy on the shoulder. "Did you need something, or just come inside to say hello?"

Toby slapped one hand against his thigh. "Oh. I almost forgot. I saw the bus. The bus is coming."

Trace glanced at the round clock hanging on the wall. "Go ahead. Zoey knows you're meeting the bus. She'll be waiting for you."

"You want me to bring her over here now. Right?"

"That's right. Grandma's not at the house today. Bring Zoey to the clinic. She can help you with the puppies."

"Okay." The boy's narrow eyes swerved to Cheyenne. "Are you Doc's new girlfriend?"

Cheyenne balked at the awkward question, but Trace took it in stride. "No romance in the clinic, remember?"

"Oh, yeah. Now I do." Toby shrugged, his wide flaccid shoulders arching high above his ears. "But she sure is pretty, ain't she?"

"Isn't she?" Trace asked.

Toby's head bobbled. "Yeah. She sure is. Even prettier than Miss Margo."

Trace laughed.

Allowing a small smile as the endearing boy shuffled out the back door, Cheyenne couldn't help wondering:

Who was Miss Margo?

Less than ten minutes and one vaccination later, Toby returned, leading an exquisite little girl by the hand.

Around eight years old, the child was fine-boned and delicate. Cheyenne assumed this was Zoey, Trace's daughter, though they shared little resemblance. Where Trace had an outdoor tan and sun-bleached brown hair that he wore short

71

and spiky, the little girl was as naturally dark as Cheyenne. Her black hair was long and pulled straight back from an intelligent café au lait forehead with a stretchy headband. Where her father's eyes were the pure blue of a June sky, Zoey's were cobalt blue and rimmed in raven lashes.

"Here she is, Doc Bowman," Toby said. "Safe and sound."

"I knew I could depend on you, Toby."

A proud smile lit the boy's moon face as he shuffled out of the room toward the kennels.

Dr. Bowman, who had barely slowed down all day, dropped what he was doing and went to the child. "How's my Zoey girl?"

Zoey lifted her arms. Trace pulled her up for a growling bear hug. Arms circling her father's neck, the little girl kissed him on the cheek with a loud smacking sound. "How's my daddy boy?"

"Beat like a drum."

Zoey pounded both palms against his shoulders in tom-tom fashion. "Like a snare drum."

This must have been a regular routine between the father and daughter because a silly exchange went on for a few more seconds. Then Trace lowered Zoey to his side and glanced toward Cheyenne.

"I want you to meet someone."

The child's face titled up toward her dad.

"More puppies to go with Frog and Toad?"

"Not animals. A real live person. But she's the one who brought us Frog and Toad."

Zoey remained politely interested, though any child would prefer puppies to people. "Who is it?"

Trace placed his hands on Zoey's shoulders and turned her toward Cheyenne.

"Zoey, this is Cheyenne, my new assistant. Cheyenne, meet my daughter. She's seven."

"Almost eight," the little girl corrected.

"Hello, Zoey, who is almost eight." Cheyenne smiled down. The child's gaze never connected with Cheyenne's, but her smile was wide and pleasant.

"She sounds nice, Daddy, like a grown-up but not old like Miss Ida June. Is she pretty, too?"

"Very pretty, Zoey. Her hair is black like yours."

"Like Mommy's was?"

Trace cleared his throat. "Yes, like Mommy's, too."

"Are her eyes blue like ours?"

Trace shot Cheyenne a pleading look as if to ask indulgence for this open discussion of her appearance. "No. They're brown."

With a wistful sigh, Zoey said, "I wish I knew what brown looked like."

Helpless sadness shrouded Trace's expression.

Then the seed that had been growing inside

73

Cheyenne's thoughts sprouted with a sudden and painful certainty.

The exquisite little Zoey was blind.

Trace held his breath, waiting for Cheyenne's reaction. Most people were kind, but Zoey had suffered through more than one condescending soul who assumed she was either deaf or stupid in addition to being visually impaired. She wasn't. Her hearing was exceptional and she was smart, insightful and absolutely gifted with animals. If she could see, she would make a great vet.

At the last thought, his stomach tightened. *If she could see.*

Cheyenne Rhodes's expression never altered. She went down on one jean-clad knee in front of Zoey, and placed a light-fingered touch on each of Zoey's forearms.

"Well, Zoey," she said, "brown is like chocolate pudding."

Zoey's interested was piqued. So was his.

"It is?"

"Do you like chocolate pudding?"

"Yes! My grandma makes the best, best pudding ever."

Cheyenne's smile was in her voice. "Then you'd like the color brown. Brown is smooth and rich and warm to the eyes in the same way chocolate pudding is to your tongue."

A light went on behind his daughter's sightless eyes. With wonder and excitement and hands extended, she spun toward Trace. "Dad, I know what brown is."

"I guess you do." He gripped her small fingers as he raised grateful eyes to his new employee and mouthed, "Thanks."

Cheyenne hitched one shoulder in dismissal, but Trace held her gaze with his, longing to express his gratitude. Where Zoey was concerned he took no effort lightly. In thirty seconds, his new employee had done something he'd never known how to do. She'd given Zoey her first glimpse of color.

Behind the pretty face and aloof demeanor, Cheyenne Rhodes was more than a wounded bird for Redemption's healing waters. She was a very interesting woman.

Wouldn't the town matchmakers go wild if they heard him say that?

Three days later, Trace was finishing up another hectic twelve-hour day. What he hoped was the last of his patients had just left and Zoey had arrived, full of excitement about the elementary school's spring concert. While restocking supplies, Cheyenne was patiently listening to his daughter rattle on and on about learning to play "If You're Happy and You Know It" on the recorder.

"And some of the other kids who don't play recorder will stomp their feet like this." Zoey marched out a three-beat rhythm. "It's gonna be awesome. Will you come?"

Cheyenne was quiet for a moment and the muscles in Trace's neck tightened. "Sure. I'd like to hear you play."

Trace let out the breath he didn't know he was holding. He didn't care one way or the other if Cheyenne attended Zoey's concert, but he didn't want his daughter disappointed.

"Someday I'm going to play piano and flute and violin and everything. I might even be on TV and be famous."

Cheyenne's soft laugh turned him around. He caught her eye and smiled. "My daughter the virtuoso."

Her eyebrows flicked. "You never know."

He still hadn't cracked the secret code of Cheyenne Rhodes, but he had figured out a few things about her. Though she presented a tough facade, she had a kind heart. She was gentle with the animals, and if not particularly warm to their owners, at least polite. She treated Toby and Zoey as if they were worthwhile people with something to add to the world. Not everyone did. And with Cheyenne, the kindness didn't seem to be an effort. She was real.

She was also a quick study and didn't back away from anything he asked her to do in the clinic. She might flinch, but she didn't back down.

He knew she'd taken an apartment at Kitty's motel, but other than work, she hadn't been seen around town. G. I. Jack and Popbottle Jones made certain he knew that much. They seemed compelled to remind him that his civic and Christian duty included introducing her to Redemption.

He knew them well enough to recognize their less than subtle efforts to test the romantic waters. They did so with every single woman in town. Why should Cheyenne escape their machinations?

They conveniently ignored the fact that he and Margo were considered an item. Not that he was particularly happy about the erroneous assumption, but he simply hadn't had the time or the emotional energy to put a stop to a dead-end relationship.

With a rueful twist of his mouth, he shook his head. He wasn't too proud of himself. Margo deserved better.

"Dr. Bowman." Jeri stuck her head around the edge of the wall. Her colorful beads and bright, cheery face brought a smile. "Pastor Parker's on the phone. One of his daughter's ewes is having trouble."

"There goes my quiet night in front of the tube."

Jeri snorted. She knew as well as he did that a quiet spring evening was an anomaly for a country vet.

Pastor Parker's daughter was a good hand with her sheep. If Kylie was calling, the ewe was in more trouble than the young teen could handle.

"Tell them I'm on my way."

"Will do, and Margo called earlier. Said to call her back."

Trace grimaced. This was the second call today that he'd forgotten to return and he dreaded looking at his cell messages. He rarely answered his cell phone during business hours and never when he was in surgery. Margo would not be happy.

"Thanks. I'll call her on the way." To Cheyenne and Zoey, he said, "Looks like we're having a baby lamb tonight. Want to go with me?"

Zoey leaped into the air, hands clapping. "Yes, yes, yes!"

Cheyenne didn't answer, so Trace tried again, this time focusing on her. "I may need your help."

An overstatement, but Popbottle Jones's exhortation still rang in his mind; plus Trace had this unfathomable need to spend some one-on-one with his new employee. Maybe the Lord was prompting him. After all, the sheep belonged to the preacher. Shouldn't he take any opportunity to introduce newcomers to the pastor?

Still, Cheyenne hesitated, looking around as if an excuse was hard to find but she needed one.

"Overtime pay," he coaxed. "Maybe even a burger."

Zoey reached out, her graceful hands searching the air until she found Cheyenne's arm. "The baby lambs are so soft. Have you ever held a lamb?"

"No, I can't say that I have."

"Wouldn't you like to? They're really, really cute, and they won't bite. If you get scared, I'll be right there with you. Lambs like me."

Cheyenne's face softened. "I don't doubt that one bit."

"So you'll go with us? I'm a good assistant but you have eyes."

Cheyenne's tough facade melted. Zoey had a special way with all kinds of living creatures, including one standoffish female.

"How can I refuse?"

"Then it's decided," Trace said, a sudden rush of happy endorphins flushing through his system. "Let me tell the others to close the clinic, and we'll be off."

Zoey clapped her hands again, a soft pitter-pattering like butterfly wings. She reached for Cheyenne. "You've made me the happiest girl in the whole wide world."

Cheyenne raised amused eyes to his and laughed. "Exaggeration will get you anywhere."

Zoey's charm machine was turned on today. Maybe she, like he, felt trouble bubbling beneath the surface of Cheyenne Rhodes and wanted to help. Or maybe she simply liked the woman. Cheyenne had paid more attention to his daughter in the past few days than Margo ever had, that was for sure.

The thought caught him up short. Margo was good to Zoey. She babysat any time he asked, though he tried never to take advantage. Why was he suddenly down on her?

He glanced at his new assistant.

The change couldn't have anything to do with Cheyenne. Could it?

Trace drove a big six-wheel pickup with double doors and a camper shell on back to cover a myriad of tools. Dried mud splattered the fender wells and halfway up the doors labeled with the clinic's name and phone number. As if Trace needed to advertise.

Cheyenne liked the truck on sight. The dually had strength and character—like its owner.

Troubled by thoughts that seemed determined to focus on Trace, she motioned to Zoey and then caught herself. Zoey's amazing ability to maneuver about the clinic and its grounds without help caused Cheyenne to forget the little girl was blind. Tonight, she'd followed her father out the back door with a long white cane, through the kennels where she'd stopped to scratch a few eager heads and now stood patiently beside the truck.

"Front or back?" Cheyenne gazed down at the

placid, beautiful child, a hitch beneath her ribs.

"In the back please. My stuff is back there."

Cheyenne opened the rear passenger door, wanting to help but not knowing exactly what she should do. Zoey's slender fingers found the metal sides. She gingerly lifted one sneaker-clad foot and hoisted herself expertly into the backseat.

As Cheyenne slammed the door, she spotted Zoey's "stuff." Some toys, a CD player, some books. The last made her curious. How did Zoey read books? Did she know Braille already?

Trace came around behind her. "All set?"

"Ready."

He reached for the passenger door, a simple gesture of good manners, but she clambered inside and yanked the door shut. What was the matter with her that she couldn't accept a simple, courteous gesture from anyone?

No, not anyone. An attractive man.

After a second, in which Trace looked bewildered and a little embarrassed, he jogged around the front of the truck and climbed inside.

"Sorry about the mess. I never have time to clean," he said, indicating gloves, papers, syringes and a collection of opened and unopened medication boxes. "Move any junk out of your way."

She'd seen police cars that looked the same way. "Work on wheels is never tidy. Don't worry about it."

Some women were finicky. She wasn't one of them.

He cranked the engine and put the truck into gear, all the while stabbing one finger at his cell phone. "Excuse me while I return this call. I'll only need a minute."

They pulled out onto Mercy Street. She never failed to notice that street sign.

"Driving and talking is dangerous," she muttered. It should also be illegal.

Trace flashed a grin and started to say something when apparently his call was answered.

"Margo? Trace. What's up?"

Cheyenne turned her head to stare out the side window and pretend she couldn't hear the personal conversation.

By the vet's terse, conciliatory replies, he was in hot water with the woman named Margo.

Her interest was piqued, but she strained not to listen, focusing on the quaint little town instead with its rows of tidy Victorian homes, pretty yards and flower-lined sidewalks. Bright yellow daffodils were in full flower as were scarlet tulips and purple redbuds. Fat robins hopped on green lawns.

Renewal was everywhere. She hoped some of it landed on her.

"Look, Margo." Trace's normally calm voice had gone tight with annoyance. "I said I was

82

sorry. You know what I do for a living. Especially this time of year. Right. Okay. That's probably a good idea."

With that, the flip phone snapped shut and bounced onto the dash. Whoa. Dr. Pollyanna had lost his smile.

Cheyenne tried to look anywhere but at Trace. This was none of her business. She shouldn't have overheard a personal conversation, but she couldn't help feeling defensive for him.

She slid a glance in his direction. Knuckles white against the steering wheel, Trace stared straight ahead at the curving road, face set in a tight expression.

An uncomfortable silence extended until Zoey leaned over the backseat. "Is Margo mad at you, Daddy?"

Trace blew out a gusty sigh. "My fault. Nothing for you to worry about."

Zoey patted her father's shoulder. "She shouldn't be mad. You didn't do anything. 'Sides, I'm glad she didn't come with us."

"I thought you liked Margo."

The child hitched a shoulder. "She's nice and she makes good peanut butter cookies. But I don't like for her to make you upset. I like Cheyenne better."

Trace rolled an embarrassed glance toward Cheyenne. "Sorry about that. Margo is a friend of mine."

Zoey poked her head over the seat. "Girl-friend," she corrected.

Trace tapped her forehead with one backward reaching finger. "Only a friend. A friend who doesn't like to be ignored."

"Margo likes Daddy for more than a friend. She told me. I don't think Daddy wants to marry her, though. I hope not."

Trace groaned. He patted the top of her head. "Okay, pumpkin, enough information."

The man's workload was grueling. Any woman who had a thing for the good-looking vet would have to deal with that or stay upset all the time.

"You've been pretty busy."

"Spring is the busiest." He rubbed a hand over the back of his neck, an action she'd seen him do plenty of times, usually following a particu-larly exhausting procedure. The vet was tired, and having some woman on his case didn't help.

"Why spring?"

"Babies. Sheep, cows, horses. Animals give birth in spring and birthing brings plenty of other problems along with it." He flipped on the turn indicator. "Pastor Parker lives down this road about a mile. His daughter raises show sheep."

"Does your work ever slow down?"

"A country vet stays as busy as he wants to year-round, especially the ones like me who see farm animals as well as pets."

"Being the only vet, you don't have much choice, do you?"

"Oh, sure, I have a choice, but how do I say no? The loss of one farm animal is significant to my clients. And if all farms stopped producing animals, what are the rest of us going to eat?"

"Veggies?" she asked with a smile.

He widened his blue, blue eyes in mock horror. "Woman, watch your mouth. This is cattle country. The only vegetarians are the animals themselves!"

Cheyenne laughed and marveled at the sound. When was the last time she'd laughed with such ease? Maybe Redemption was having a positive effect on her. Or maybe the reason was the handsome veterinarian.

She turned the idea over in her head, then left it there. A few days in his company and she was laughing again. That much at least was good. As long as she didn't get any romantic notions in her crazy head, she'd be fine.

"Thanks," she said.

Trace's look was quizzical. "For?"

She shrugged. "Nothing. Everything."

The front wheel of the truck jounced into a pothole, tossing Cheyenne sideways, close enough to brush elbows with her boss. She braced a hand on the dash and pushed back.

Trace made a left-hand turn, casting her an amused look. "Spoken like a true female. No wonder we men have this stupid expression on our faces all the time."

She wouldn't consider anything about him stupid, especially that face. Trace Bowman just might be one of the good guys. A couple of years ago, he would have been her type. Now she didn't have a type. Couldn't ever have one again.

As if she'd swallowed a brick, heaviness settled in her stomach. She'd come to Redemption for peace and escape, not for a man. Best to remember that.

"Is this the preacher's house?"

A two-story brick home sat at the end of a short driveway.

"This is it." He pulled into a grassy parking area next to a beat-up truck and a bronze SUV. A battered church bus was parked up ahead next to a garagelike structure.

They slammed out of the truck. Trace took Zoey's hand and the three of them started toward the house. Halfway there, a shout from behind turned them around.

"We're out here, Doc." A sturdy blonde woman in brown coveralls and work boots waved from a barn door.

The trio crossed the wide space between house and barn. Thick clover sprouted in dark patches among the grass and put off a sweet, fresh scent. The barn was fairly new, painted red, but built in the older triangular style with a hay loft above.

Inside, the smell was springtime, dust and hay.

A preteen girl with a blond ponytail, clearly the offspring of the woman, waved them into a stall. Her young face was tense with worry.

"She's been in labor too long, Doc. I felt for the lamb and it seems in the right position but Betsy can't deliver."

"Let me see what we have."

After a quick introduction to Kylie, the young sheep owner, and her mother, Michelle Parker, Cheyenne moved to the corner of the stall to watch, wondering why Trace had bothered to bring her along. She was useless here. Even Zoey was more useful. The little girl positioned herself on the mound of straw in front of the ewe, gently stroking the mother sheep's forehead while she murmured something unintelligible.

After a thorough hand wash, Trace examined the ewe, talking quietly to both owners and sheep.

"That's a big lamb for a young mother," he said softly.

"Can we save them?" The preteen Kylie was matter-of-fact, as Cheyenne supposed a farm girl had to be about livestock, but her eyes were glassy with leashed tears. "I've raised Betsy from a lamb. She took grand champion at the fair this year."

From his position on his knees leaning over the ewe, Trace winked at the young girl. "Let's turn this fat lady over on her back and see what we can do to help. Kylie, you and Zoey keep her calm and quiet while I do the hard stuff. Okay?"

Kylie nodded, ponytail bobbing as she helped the vet reposition the ewe. Their ministrations were met with a plaintive *baaa,* but in minutes, Dr. Bowman had somehow done what neither the ewe nor her owners could accomplish. A wet lamb slipped into his hands. He gave the infant a quick swing by its front feet and placed the slick body on the hay in front of the mother. When the lamb began to wiggle, they breathed a collective sigh.

"It's a girl," Kylie said. "Betsy's little trouble-maker."

"Typical female," Trace teased, hands on his hips as he grinned around at the gathered group of females.

"Be careful, Doc, you're surrounded."

Hands raised in surrender, he laughed, teeth flashing white against tanned skin and a five-o'clock scruff. Trace Bowman was at home in his own skin. And he had an ease with people that Cheyenne could respect. She'd had that once. Getting it back wouldn't be easy.

"Before I get in too much trouble, I'd better finish my job and get out of here," he said.

Following a further exam of both ewe and lamb, instinct took over and the lamb began to nurse.

A warm, peaceful feeling spread through Cheyenne's body. She was glad she'd come along. There was something beautiful and confirming in seeing a living creature born. And if there was one thing she needed, it was to find the wonder of living again instead of the ugliness.

"Let's go inside and have some pie and coffee before you go," Michelle Parker said to Trace.

"I'm staying out here with Betsy, Mom," the girl named Kylie said.

"Me, too, Daddy." Zoey remained beside the ewe. "Can I stay with Kylie?"

Trace lifted an eyebrow toward the preteen, who nodded. "She can come when I do. I'll look out for her."

"All right, then." To Mrs. Parker he said, "Coffee sounds good."

He tossed equipment back into a bag. Cheyenne stooped to help and was rewarded with a grin. Her heart flip-flopped.

"We'll pass on the pie," Trace was saying. "No dinner yet."

"I can fix you a sandwich," the pastor's wife said as they all fell into step and headed toward the house.

"Thanks, but I promised Cheyenne and Zoey one of Big Bob's Angus burgers and curly fries."

Cheyenne blinked. He had?

Behind Michelle's back, he winked at Cheyenne, and even though she quickly averted her gaze, a glimmer of sunshine settled inside her chest. She'd already been feeling mellow and now she was actually relaxed enough to enjoy herself. What a concept.

As they entered the kitchen through the back door, the pastor's wife turned her attention to Cheyenne. "You must be new in town. I don't think I've seen you around."

"Brand-new, as of about a week ago."

"And Trace already has you making after-hours calls." The woman made a teasing *tsk-tsk* in Trace's direction. "Slave driver."

He scraped a chair away from a gleaming oak table and sat down, comfortable as though he came here often. "I told her when I hired her that I'm a desperate man."

True, but she hadn't believed him. Now, after working with him inside and outside the clinic, she understood.

Taking a chair opposite him, she allowed a casual look around. The Parkers' kitchen was a combination of country warmth and modern convenience. She could imagine happy meals in this room. She'd grown up in a home like this, where family mattered and hours around the kitchen table had resolved the problems and struggles of her teenage years.

But her family's table had grown quieter after

Mom's death, fading to silence in the past year. She didn't blame Dad and Brent. They simply did not know what to say or do anymore. But she'd struggled alone, in silence, until she could bear it no longer.

She bit down on the inside of her cheek and concentrated on that one small pain. Anything to get her mind off Colorado.

Michelle handed out fragrant cups of coffee, motioning toward sugar and cream in the center of the table. Coffee around the Parker table must be a common affair. "So, where are you from, Cheyenne?"

The question was a normal one. Hadn't she asked the same thing of others many times?

Eyes on the curl of steam rising from her cup, she said, "Colorado."

"Beautiful state. What brings you here?"

Good question. And one she couldn't answer without spilling her guts to strangers.

Trace's mug thumped against the table. "Where's Pastor Parker? I wanted to introduce him."

Bless Trace. Whether he knew it or not, he'd rescued her. She flicked a glance his way. He was watching her, eyes crinkling at the corners.

"Great coffee, huh?" he said innocently, a smile playing around his lips.

"Terrific." Was she so transparent that her employer had already figured out she had something to hide? For months after the garage attack she'd wondered if people could tell what had happened just by looking at her. She knew now that the thoughts were paranoid, part of post-traumatic stress, but still they came back to haunt her on a regular basis.

Could Trace tell? Did he pity her? Or worse, judge her?

To quiet the swarm of irrational thoughts, she took a swallow of hot coffee. The liquid burned her tongue and throat but had the desired effect.

If Michelle Parker noticed anything strange about her visitor, she was a master of discretion.

"Rob ran over to check on Ida June. She took another fall."

"Ida June Click is our octogenarian handy-woman," he said to Cheyenne. "She's always into something."

"She's still working?" And as handywoman, no less?

"According to Ida June, the day she quits working is the day the Lord will call her home. Idle hands are the devil's workshop." Michelle smiled above the rim of her cup. "That's a direct quote."

"What was she doing this time?" Trace asked. "Installing another ceiling fan for an 'old person'?"

"Worse. She was repairing the guttering on one of her rent houses. The old gutter pulled loose and down she came."

"Is she hurt?"

"According to Ida June, the only thing hurt is her pride. Rob said she had a goose egg bruise on her forehead and was mad as a wet cat, but she refused to let him drive her to the doctor."

"That's Ida June. And if I don't miss my guess, she'll be at church on Sunday ready to teach her class."

"No doubt about it. The day she misses church is the day after she moves to heaven. Forsake not the assembling. That's another direct quote." Smiling fondly, Michelle set her coffee down. "What about you, Cheyenne? Have you found a church yet? We'd love to have you attend Redemption Fellowship."

The tension, momentarily soothed by the story of Ida June, crept back in. Cheyenne shook her head. "I'm not much on church attendance. But thank you for the invitation."

As far as she could tell, she wasn't God's favorite child. She hadn't lived a perfect life, but no one deserved to be punished like that. Where was God the night Dwight Hector broke into her garage?

The room grew quiet except for a single gurgle of the coffeepot. "Well, if you change your mind, the door is always open."

"Nice to know."

But she wouldn't change her mind.

Chapter Six

C✑

T race was feeling pretty good as he polished
off the remnants of a super-deluxe Angus
burger with a basket of curly fries and listened
to Cheyenne and Zoey jokingly bicker over the
merits of mustard versus ketchup.

This was the third time in two weeks he'd been
called out while Cheyenne was on duty and he'd
brought her along. This was also the third time
he'd insisted on buying burgers afterward.

Cheyenne was becoming an able assistant and
he needed her on these calls. At least that's what
he told himself. And she didn't seem to mind
tagging along. Behind the tough-girl facade,
Cheyenne's emotions were not easy to read.

She and Zoey got on well, too. In fact,
Cheyenne was more relaxed with Zoey than she
was with him.

Why that mattered to him, he wasn't sure just
yet. The Lord was up to something where
Cheyenne was concerned, but he hadn't figured
out what he was supposed to do about it. When
Michelle Parker had mentioned church,
Cheyenne had thrown up a roadblock faster
than he could give a rabies injection.

But then, sometimes ministry was more than church. In fact, most of the time Trace was more comfortable sharing his faith in nonreligious situations. In his opinion, the day-to-day living, with God in the lead, drew people to Christ, not church attendance. Religion had caused him plenty of trouble in the past. God, on the other hand, was faithful. But he'd struggled a long time to figure that out and had blamed God for every problem.

Maybe Cheyenne was in the same boat.

He pointed a limp curl of potato at her. "Have you had a chance to see much of the town since you've been here?"

She lifted one eyebrow and said dryly, "I keep hours with you, remember?"

He grinned. "Guilty as charged."

"Which means I'm on a first-name basis with a lot of animals and a handful of owners who think you are the world's greatest vet."

"The owners are easier to persuade than their pets."

Cheyenne chuckled and Trace's stomach lifted in happy response. Why did something as simple as a throaty laugh give him such pleasure?

"So, no, to answer your question. My explorations of Redemption have been limited by my workaholic boss."

"Then I know just what the doctor will order.

A genuine, five-star, escorted and narrated tour of the city's hot spots."

"Redemption has hot spots?" she asked doubtfully, one eyebrow arched in wry humor.

"Probably somewhere," he said, feeling good to know he'd put the sparkle into those dark brown eyes. He was starting to understand her sense of humor. Behind the aloof attitude that kept her walled off from other people, Cheyenne wielded a dry wit and a razor-sharp mind. "But Zoey keeps a tight rein on her old dad. No hot spots for Dr. Daddy."

"Oh, Daddy, you're funny," Zoey said, swirling a fry round and round in ketchup. "Daddy's good with the tour, Cheyenne. You'll like it."

"The tour? Are you moonlighting, Doc? Vet by day, official Redemption tour guide by night?"

He liked when she teased him. "Official tour guides would be G. I. Jack and Popbottle Jones. They know every alley, every creek, every house and the people in them."

She pointed a straw at him. "And what's in their trash cans, too?"

"Especially the trash cans." He returned the point, slashing across the end of her straw with a fencing motion. She battled him for a few thrusts until his straw bent.

"Oops. Sorry."

"No, you're not."

She shrugged, but the sparkle in her eyes gave him hope. Somewhere behind that defensive facade was a really fun woman. He was sure of it.

"So what's the decision? Want the tour? Might as well accept. I'm relentless."

"Don't you ever sleep?"

"Tonight will be a quiet night. I feel it in my bones."

"Last time Daddy said that, he took me to Grandma's at ten and stayed gone all night."

Trace reached over and tweaked Zoey's nose. "Tattletale. Whose side are you on anyway?"

"Yours. And Cheyenne's." The delicate face swiveled in Cheyenne's direction, though her eyes never made contact. "Say yes. It's easier. Daddy's not good with the word *no*."

Cheyenne, soda straw to her lips, set the cup down abruptly and sputtered with laughter.

Trace, grinning, waited until she regained her composure to say, "She's right, you know. I don't take rejection well. And you are my employee."

"Is that blackmail?"

"Pure and simple. So what will it be, the fifty-cent tour or the dollar one?"

Cheyenne reached into her jeans pocket, pulled out a wadded bill and slapped it on the table. "I'm feeling reckless. Let's go for the whole buck."

Spring brought more hours of sunlight, but the weather was cool and Cheyenne was glad for her jacket. The tour, as Trace and Zoey called their excursion, included a drive to the river bridge she'd admired her first day in town. She'd been meaning to come back and explore once she was settled, but hadn't the time or inclination. Seeing the pretty old bridge with Trace and Zoey appealed more than it should.

Zoey Bowman was adorable, a gifted child whose lack of vision did nothing to dampen her joie de vivre. Cheyenne had wondered for days what happened to her eyesight. She'd also wondered about Zoey's mother, but some things were too personal to ask. If Trace still grieved for his wife, she didn't want to pry and stir up painful memories. Besides, she didn't want anyone prying into her life. Why should she pry into theirs?

But she did wonder.

"This is a place everyone should see," Trace was saying. "Without the river and this bridge for crossing, there would never have been a town called Redemption."

He pulled the truck off the road and parked beneath a stand of willows at the end of the bridge where stone met earth.

"It looks old. Pretty, but old."

"The bridge *is* old. Well, half the structure is.

98

The other lane is an imitation built in modern times to match, but this side is still the original stone constructed for wagons and horses."

The cop in her had to ask, "Is it safe?"

Trace shrugged as if he never worried about safety. Life must have treated him well in that respect. He was lucky.

"The county does the upkeep, but since the bridge is on the list of historical structures, I don't know how they do it. But every part of the road, including the bridge, has to pass inspection or be closed. I'm certain it's as safe as any."

"Can we get out and look around?"

Zoey was already unbuckling her seat belt.

Trace reached for his. "I'd be a poor tour guide if I kept you trapped in a truck."

An unexpected shiver wiggled up the back of her neck. Trapped in a vehicle. Not a good thought. A dark image rose behind her eyelids.

"If you look through those trees," Trace was saying, "you can see where Redemption River curves toward town."

Cheyenne shook off the tremor of anxiety and firmly blocked the images kaleidoscoping inside her head. The flashbacks hadn't come in a long time. She wasn't about to let them start again.

Unclicking her seat belt, she hopped outside, gripping the hard metal of the door.

The breeze was soft on her skin, whispering affirmations of life and safety. She was okay.

Everything was fine. Tree leaves rustled. A car motored past. An insect droned nearby.

Normal sounds in the here and now.

"Cheyenne?"

She opened her eyes to find Trace standing two feet away, peering at her with concern.

"Want to walk down to the bank?"

Cheyenne took a deep, cleansing breath and let the air out slowly, somehow finding a weak smile. The man must think she was nuts to stand here on the side of the road with her eyes closed, gripping a truck door for dear life.

"Is someone fishing down there?" Even to her own ears, her voice sounded thready and strange.

After watching her for one final, frowning moment—enough to let her know he'd noticed something was amiss—Trace shaded his eyes and looked through the lace of green leaves and grass toward the riverbank.

"Looks like G. I. Jack and Popbottle Jones. Want to go down and say hello?"

Zoey tugged on her father's hand. "Yes, Daddy. Let's go. Come on, Cheyenne. Come on!"

Zoey's enthusiasm was infectious, and Cheyenne couldn't resist the special little girl. Never once had she heard the child complain about her handicap. The world could take a lesson from this seven-going-on-eight-year-old.

"I paid a dollar for this tour," she said, forcing

cheer into the words. "Might as well get my money's worth."

They headed down a sharp, grassy incline, skidding a little as they went. When she began to slide, Cheyenne reached for a tree limb, but Trace caught her elbow first. His grip, strong from work with large animals, held her steady.

She seldom let anyone touch her intentionally, but she didn't pull away. Instead of feeling threatened, she was comforted by his strength.

She must be hallucinating.

"The river is always stinky down here," Zoey said, nose wrinkled as she sniffed in a noisy rush of air. "But I like it."

"This from a child raised in a veterinary clinic." Humor crinkled the skin around Trace's eyes.

"Oh, Daddy, puppies smell good. The clinic doesn't stink."

This time, Trace laughed. "That's why God sent you to be my daughter."

"And it's a good thing, too, huh, Daddy?"

"A very good thing. Couldn't live through the day without my Zoey. You're my best girl."

Zoey tilted her head in a knowing gesture. "Margo thinks *she's* your best girl."

Trace flicked a glance at Cheyenne, but his expression was unreadable. Quietly, he said, "Margo's only a friend. You and I have talked about that before."

His reply sent a burst of energy zipping along Cheyenne's nerve endings. She tried to tamp back the rush of emotion, but, good or bad, there it was. She was glad Trace Bowman wasn't married or involved.

Biting hard on her bottom lip, she pretended to focus on the trail ahead, but her mind was on Trace Bowman, on the soft denial, on the way his powerful fingers steadied her elbow, on the kindness he'd shown her since their first meeting.

That was it. Kindness. Like a dog that had been kicked and starved for attention, she was responding to this man's innate kindness. That was what this rush of feeling was all about. Kindness. Nothing more.

There was nothing else left for a woman like her.

"I can walk the rest of the way without help," she said, abruptly pulling her arm from his grasp.

Trace shot her a look of surprise but didn't argue when she held back, letting him go ahead.

Zoey held tight to her daddy's other arm, feeling her way with her sneakered feet. Trace moved patiently, giving her time, though Cheyenne thought the little girl was amazingly confident.

When they reached the bottom of the incline, Trace glanced back at her. "Okay?"

"Fine." She skidded the last few feet and made her way toward the shoreline. Something in

Trace's questioning glance made her regret her edginess. Why did she have to be so jumpy? The man was kindness personified. Not a threat. Except maybe to her heart. She might be crazy, but she wasn't stupid enough to fall in love again.

"The water is red," she said, more for something to say than because she cared.

Trace touched her elbow but as if recalling her rejection a few moments ago, let his hand fall to his side. Cheyenne experienced a quiver of both relief and disappointment.

"Different from the clear streams of Colorado, I guess," his warm baritone said. "A lot of Oklahoma dirt is red, so our rivers tend to be reddish. When old Jonas Case settled here, the river was the main reason. I don't think he cared one bit if the water was red and muddy. Water was life."

"I've never given history much thought, but toting water from a river every day for laundry or dishes or drinking—for everything—must have been difficult."

Cheyenne's thoughts were anywhere but on history and a muddy river named Redemption. Trace was an animal doctor, a nurturer, a healer. Touching was as natural for him as breathing. She shouldn't read anything into a simple touch on the elbow.

An emotional wreck, that was what she was. Being with normal people who didn't know about her was a stark reminder of just how different she was now. If Trace knew, he wouldn't touch her. Like Paul, he'd try to be kind but he'd soon pull away, using lame excuses. He had a meeting. He had to work out. His mother had called.

In the end, when the excuses were gone, so was he.

"Jonas and his friends dug a well at the town's center," Trace said.

What was he talking about? Oh, right, water, the river, the first settlers.

"A central well made life a little easier. But old Jonas believed in baptizin', as he called it. So he'd haul new converts out here every Sunday in his wagon, whether they wanted to come or not, and dunk them until they shouted hallelujah."

"And what did he do if they didn't shout hallelujah?"

"Drowned them."

Cheyenne laughed in spite of herself. "No, he didn't."

Trace's eyes twinkled. "The Old West was a wild time and from all reports, old Jonas had been a wild man. You never know." Sobering, he pointed downstream. "Some folks claimed the water washed all their problems down the river and right out into the Atlantic Ocean."

"Do you believe that stuff?"

"Do I believe the water washed away their trouble? No. Nothing special in the water. But I believe God can repair whatever's broken inside a person. I'm living proof."

She blinked at the easy admission. "Seriously? You seem so—" she shrugged "—I don't know. Together, I guess."

He gave a derisive snort. "God's still working on me. But when I first came to Redemption I was a mess with a capital *M*. Old Jonas Case would have drowned me in this river for sure."

The hardworking, kindhearted Trace Bowman, a mess? Like her? No way.

She wanted to hear more, but by now they were nearing the ragtag pair of old men who stood on the bank, fishing lines dangling in the gurgling waters. Before Cheyenne could pry into Trace's private life, one of the men called out.

"Ahoy, there! Is that the doc and little Zoey?"

Trace lifted a hand in greeting. "It is."

"Who's that with you? Cheyenne Rhodes?"

Trace and Cheyenne exchanged glances.

"How did he know?"

Trace widened his eyes as if to say he had no clue. "Yes, sir, this is her. We're taking the tour."

"Well, come on over and say howdy. Me and Popbottle was just talking about our new lady in town. Wasn't we, Popbottle?"

"Indeed. Had we not seen you, we would have

inquired tomorrow at the clinic about her well-being."

Why would two old bums care about her?

The bank was damp and her boots sank slightly into the mud as she approached the odd pair. Gingerly, she lifted her boot for a look.

Trace noticed and said, "Beats what I slog through every day."

She made a face. He grinned.

Trace Bowman had the best grin, one of those eye-squinting, dimple-deepening, full-faced grins that could charm anyone into anything. Like Paul Ramos.

She dropped her boot to the ground and sighed.

Don't go getting distracted, Cheyenne. Men are men.

Behind the fisherman, two rewoven lawn chairs were perched a few feet from the water. An old metal box, the hinges wired together, hung open like a wide mouth pouring out fishing lures, red and white floats, shiny gold hooks.

"Catching anything?" Trace asked.

"Not a bite all afternoon." Popbottle Jones sounded as chipper as if he'd caught a truckful.

"Why are you still at it?"

"Fishing and prayer go together like bologna and cheese." G. I. Jack made the statement as though it made sense.

Cheyenne studied the older fellow with interest. Wearing his usual bedraggled army cap and jacket, he hadn't shaved in a while and hair sprouted from his face as well as from the sides of the cap and the tops of his ears. Today, a slice of pizza protruded from his shirt pocket. Pepperoni.

"What my compatriot means is that a man can solve many problems with a fishing rod in hand, the sun warming his back and the Lord Almighty on his shoulder." Popbottle Jones placed a light hand on Zoey's hair. Cheyenne expected his nails to be dirty. They weren't. "Zoey, my girl, keep an eye on my line, will you please?"

Zoey giggled and took the offered fishing rod in her small hands, unoffended by the impossible request. "Popbottle says I can see with my heart."

"We all can. You're just better at it." The interesting old man squatted beside the metal box and rummaged around, coming out with a black rubber worm. "Ah, this should do the trick. No bass can resist a black worm. So tell me, Cheyenne Rhodes, how do you like our fair city?"

Hands shoved into the pockets of her jeans, Cheyenne answered, "I like it. It's quiet and peaceful."

Focused on threading the plastic worm onto a hook, he said, "A telling remark, I'm sure you realize. One who seeks peace must understand what it means to be without peace."

"Everyone needs peace and quiet," she said, a little too defensively. What was the deal with these people? Had she stumbled upon a town full of wannabe psychiatrists? Or just a bunch of religious nuts?

No, that wasn't fair. People in Redemption had gone out of their way to be kind and helpful. Just because she had a chip on her shoulder and a knot in her gut wasn't their fault.

"Have you been to the well yet?" the old man asked casually, still at work on the fishing lure.

"The well?" she asked, lifting a brow toward Trace. "The town well?"

The three men exchanged looks that Cheyenne didn't comprehend.

"Go on, Doc," G. I. Jack prodded. "Take her to see the well."

A weird feeling came over her.

What was the big deal about a well?

Chapter Seven

∽

In less than ten minutes, they'd recrossed the stone bridge and driven to the town center. A few cars puttered around the cul-de-sac and down the main thoroughfare, but Redemption was mostly quiet. Cheyenne had yet to adjust to the slow pace in a small town, though she appreciated it.

A little too aware of her boss across the seat, Cheyenne turned her face toward the town circle. "I noticed this little park the day I arrived. It's beautiful. And right here in the center of town."

"Town Square," he corrected. "Back in the Land Run days, all the businesses and homes were built around the square for safety and convenience."

"I'm glad progress didn't see fit to destroy it."

He killed the motor. "I had the same thought when I first moved here."

Seat belts clattered as they were unlatched. The sun was lowering in the west, nearing sunset, but enough daylight remained for a brief look.

Zoey was out of the cab first. "I smell flowers."

Cheyenne took a deep breath, drawing in the clean scent. "Sweet William. And lots of it."

Zoey stopped, nose in the air and sniffed loudly. "Sweet William? No one ever told me that."

Trace slammed his door but didn't bother to press the locks. Another small-town habit Cheyenne would have to get used to, though personally, she would never leave anything unlocked. Even small towns had criminals or they wouldn't need a police force.

"That's because your dad wouldn't know a sweet William from a sour Sue," Trace said.

"Oh, Daddy." To Cheyenne, Zoey said, "He's silly but I like him, don't you?"

She and Trace exchanged amused glances. Yes, she liked him, and she shouldn't. Maybe she should find another job where the boss wasn't single and charming and nice-looking. But she'd been running on survival instinct for too long, and she was tired of running, period. She liked her boss. Big deal. She'd liked Captain Boggs, too.

Okay, so that was a different kind of like. The captain had been over sixty and happily married for forty years. And Trace Bowman . . . wasn't.

"Daddy?"

"Waiting for you, pumpkin."

The child was a pleasant distraction from thinking about the father. As she rounded the vehicle, Zoey's fingertips lightly skirted the metal frame until they made contact with Trace.

"One step," Trace said. He pulled up on the little girl's arm to keep her from stumbling on the curb.

Up she went, lithely, easily, and with confidence. Trace had given her that. There was no way a blind child could be this well adjusted without great adults in her life. Trace treated Zoey as a sighted child most of the time and held her to high expectations. The result was this wonderful, resilient little girl with a killer smile and a zest for life.

A twinge of sadness tried to creep in again. She and Paul had discussed children, though he was less enthusiastic than she. They'd planned for two, one of each, but now that would never happen. Not with Paul. Not with anyone.

As they crossed the street, the smell of green spring was in the air, along with a hint of exhaust from circling cars. Most of the shops were already closed, an anomaly to a woman accustomed to the city where stores kept late hours.

Their shoes made soft taps on the stone walkway. A horn honked and Trace raised a hand in greeting.

"Pastor Parker," he said, and Cheyenne stared with interest after the passing pickup truck, though she couldn't make out the preacher.

"Want to sit on one of the benches, or roam around? When people drive past, I can tell you all the gossip about them." That one charming dimple deepened. "We have some characters in Redemption, let me tell you."

"So I've noticed," she said. "But I thought we came to see the well."

"Okay. That first. Whatever the lady wishes. After all, you did pay good money for this tour."

"I should think so. A whole dollar."

They fell in step again, their arms brushing as they walked. With concerted effort, Cheyenne put a couple of inches between them.

Touching Trace Bowman, even accidentally, was not a good idea. She liked it too much.

Up ahead, she could see the little well right in the center of the park. Covered by a simple, cone-shaped roof on stilts, the well was obviously as old as Redemption Bridge.

Zoey skipped on ahead, her white cane skittering before her, as though she could see as well as anyone. She plopped down on a bench outside the gazebo, flipped upside down, draped her legs over the back and began to hum. Her hair hung down toward the sidewalk like a black waterfall.

Trace poked a finger in her belly as they passed by. She grabbed the spot with both hands and giggled.

"Is this the original well?" Cheyenne asked.

"Hand-dug by Jonas Case himself along with a few other reformed outlaws. Says so right here on the stone."

The lettering was weathered and faded but still remarkably easy to read.

"Amazing masonry for that time period."

"The same men built the bridge. If you're interested in that kind of thing, Jonas left pretty extensive journals you can see in the Land Run Museum. The language is quaint and stilted, and he was not an educated man, but his writings put you right back in the 1880s. He described how the town was built, who came and why. Along with copies of his sermons, he even listed the Christian converts he dunked in Redemption River."

"Redemption River," she mused. What kind of redemption did people seek here? Redemption from the evil deeds they'd done? Redemption from the evils done to them? Was such a thing even possible? A yearning rose inside her.

She'd never given religion much thought, though she'd considered herself a Christian. After the encounter with Dwight Hector, she'd decided religion was all smoke and mirrors and no substance. God might be up in heaven, but He didn't hang around a tequila-shooting cop.

Trace obviously believed. But then, he hadn't walked a mile in her shoes.

She traced a finger over the top of the rectangular plaque. Encased in protective glass, the stone was etched with the date June 1889, and the names of three men. Below the names were the words *Come unto me, all ye who labor and are heavy laden, and I will give you rest.*

She could feel Trace watching her and wondered if he expected some kind of reaction to the well, the men or the scripture. She felt nothing but mild interest.

"Very interesting place," she conceded. "Someday when my boss lets me leave early, I'll check out the museum."

A beat passed before Trace said, "Anytime you want."

Cheyenne couldn't help thinking she'd disappointed him some way, but couldn't imagine how. What had he wanted her to see that she obviously hadn't? What had the two old bums expected?

"Will you be my tour guide?" she asked, trying to make up for whatever she'd done wrong.

His eyes crinkled. "Got another dollar?"

"My boss is a miser but I can probably swing it."

"Hey!" He pretended hurt. "A miser?"

"A generous miser. You've also fed me practically every day."

"Burgers and sodas." He shook his head. "We gotta do better than that next time. Redemption has a steak house, you know."

Next time. Tonight had felt almost like a date. Could she let there be a next time?

Trace pulled the truck to the parking area in back of the clinic and put the transmission out of gear, but left the motor running. Night had fallen and the kennels were in shadow, lit only by one security light and the truck's low beams. A dog appeared. His eyes glowed red in the yellow light. He woofed once.

114

"Thanks for going with me again."

Body turned sideways away from him, Cheyenne reached for the door handle, ready to leave. "Enjoyed it."

He didn't know if that was true or a nicety, but he'd take what she offered. "You want to come down to the house for a while?"

She whipped around. "What?"

Even in shadow she was pretty. Earlier, as they'd walked around the square, he'd been tempted to take hold of her hand, but something had held him back. Not since he was a teen-ager had he felt so insecure with a woman. He couldn't figure her out. Maybe the mystery was her appeal, though he doubted he was that shallow.

After seeing Margo off and on for over a year, Trace had given up on anything but friendship. Cheyenne Rhodes, on the other hand, was on his mind more than any woman had been since Pamela died. He wanted to know her better.

"Just a thought," he said, trying his best to keep the invitation casual and light. "Watch a little tube. Eat a little popcorn. Kick back. Relax. No big deal." Which it wasn't. Was it?

Holding her watch close to the dash light, she said, "It's late. I don't know. I shouldn't."

He pointed a finger at her and grinned, hoping. "At least admit you're tempted. A man has a fragile ego, you know."

115

In the shadowy lighting, her mouth curved. "Maybe."

He thumped his fist on the steering wheel. "I'll take that as a yes. You haven't really lived until you've tasted Doc Bowman's chili-cheese popcorn."

She laughed, and his stomach lifted as if he'd jumped from an airplane. Cheyenne Rhodes needed to laugh more often. And he needed to hear her.

"You think a bachelor would joke about a thing as important as his specialty snack?"

"You make chili-cheese popcorn yourself? For real?"

"You're breaking my heart, lady. Sure, I make it myself. Chili-cheese popcorn is an old family recipe passed down for generations. Well, one generation. My mom taught me. It is a very complicated procedure, mastered only by a few of the most skilled culinary artists. You'll be impressed."

Her smile widened. "How can I refuse an offer to see a genius at work?"

As lighthearted as a kid, he put the truck in gear to drive the fifty yards of gravel road between his work and his home. The low ranch-style brick house had been built by the previous vet. When Trace had arrived in Redemption to take over the practice, he'd been too devastated by Pamela's death to care where he lived. If not for Zoey, he'd have lived in the clinic. If not for his faith and his child, he might not have lived at all.

A silent prayer of gratitude welled in his heart. He'd come a long way. If he could find life and hope and joy in Redemption, anyone could. He glanced again at Cheyenne's profile. Even his lovely assistant.

As the headlights swept over the house, he pressed the garage-door opener clipped on his visor and eased the outsized truck inside. The vehicle was still rocking when Zoey hopped out and, cane swaying wildly, zoomed inside the house.

Trace killed the motor and grinned. "Potty break."

Feeling good and glad to spend more time with Cheyenne, he turned in the seat, angling his body toward her. He made no move to exit the truck. Neither did she.

He'd been working with her day and night and other than in the exam rooms, this was the first time they'd really been alone.

Cheyenne's gaze followed his daughter's trail. "She's an amazing little girl, Trace. You've done a fantastic job."

"I'm not doing anything special. Zoey's just —well, she's my little miracle."

"She's wonderful."

"Yeah. God didn't give her sight but he gave her so much more."

"Would it be rude for me to ask what happened?"

"To her vision?" At her nod, he said, "Retinopathy."

"I don't know what that is."

"Basically retinopathy is a malformation of the blood vessels of the eye that sometimes occurs in premature babies."

"Can anything be done?"

"Doctors tried, but the treatments didn't work." Every six months, he took her for checkups, praying for a new treatment. Zoey never even asked. "She was born at six and a half months. The fact that she survived is a miracle. A real miracle. Vision or not, I'm thankful." He'd lost Pamela but he could easily have lost them both.

"How much did she weigh?"

"Two and a half pounds."

"Wow." Cheyenne shivered. "Scary to think of a baby that small."

"Tell me about it." He held out one hand. The glow from the dash cast his cupped fingers in shadow. "She fit right here in my palm. Like a puppy instead of a child. I was out of my mind with fear." And grief. A shattering combination that had left him numb and empty for months afterward.

"Fear can eat you alive." Cheyenne's voice was soft, reflective, the admission revealing.

Maybe the shield of darkness gave her the courage to speak. Whatever it was, Trace didn't want her to stop.

"Sounds like the voice of experience."

She gave him a shuttered look. "Everyone is afraid of something."

He didn't know where to go with that, but a small voice inside urged him to keep talking. He didn't mind spilling his guts if the revelations helped her.

"After Pamela died," he said, "I was lost. No one knew her heart was weak until it was too late. The strain of pregnancy was too much. She suffered a massive coronary and needed surgery to survive. They delivered Zoey by C-section, hoping to save them both. Zoey made it. Pamela didn't."

"I'm sorry. I can't imagine . . ."

"That was a tough few months, let me tell you. I was devastated and scared stupid. How was I going to raise a baby—a visually impaired baby —without Pamela? I was mad at God. Mad at Pamela for leaving me. Just mad in general. I had to get away. A colleague heard about the need for a country vet in some rinky-dink little town called Redemption. I drove down to check out the place and something about it . . ."

"Redemption draws people," she said softly.

"You felt it, too?"

She shook her head. "I don't know. Kitty

Wainright said that to me on my first day in town."

"It's true, you know. People come here for a variety of reasons, lots of them because they're broken in some way. And God is waiting."

"I'm not into metaphysical hocus-pocus."

"God isn't hocus-pocus, Cheyenne. He's real and He really cares. Who's to say He can't use a small town and the people in it to help hurting people?"

"I wish forgetting was as easy as that."

Forgetting? What terrible thing had happened that she didn't want to remember?

"I never said it was easy, but God is here and He cares. I know that for a fact. If I gave you a devotional, would you read it?"

She shrugged. "I don't know. Maybe."

Though disappointed that she hadn't opened up, he felt they'd made progress somehow.

The door from the garage into the house opened. Buttery yellow light from the kitchen flowed out in a rectangle. Trace was always amused that his daughter turned on the lights.

"Are you out there, Daddy?"

"Coming, pumpkin."

The little head disappeared and the door closed, shutting off the light again.

"Maybe she's scared in there by herself."

"Zoey? No. She's waiting for dear old Dad's popcorn."

"Ah, the chili-cheese specialty. We'd better get moving."

Though she'd told him nothing concrete, Trace was feeling pretty good as he pocketed the keys and went around to open the door for Cheyenne. For once, she let him.

An inward smile filled his chest. More progress.

Without giving the action any thought, he reached for her hand to help her down from the tall chassis. Again, she let him. And the smile in his chest expanded.

She hopped to the concrete and he stepped back. "Let me turn on the overhead light," he said. "This garage is full of junk. You could break your neck in here in the dark."

He pressed the remote and heard the rumble of the garage door closing and then left Cheyenne standing in the glow of the dome light as he trotted to the wall switch.

He heard a sharp intake of breath.

"I have to get out of here."

The odd statement stopped him in his tracks.

"Let me out." She sounded scared, her voice strangled in the back of her throat.

He slapped the light switch and spun around. "Cheyenne?"

Her dark skin had paled and she was breathing hard and fast. He started toward her.

"Don't." She held out her hand in stop-sign fashion and he saw she was shaking. "Don't."

121

She was looking toward him, but she wasn't looking *at* him. It was as though she saw someone else.

Hair rose on the back of his neck. What was going on?

Eyes wide and glazed, she backed away, toward the closed garage door.

As he would with a frightened animal, Trace kept his voice soft and soothing, but moved slowly toward her. "Cheyenne? What's wrong? Talk to me."

By now, she was trembling like a wet kitten, her chest rising and falling as if she'd made ten laps around the clinic. With a strangled cry, she whirled away and pounded at the closed garage door.

"I have to get out. Let me out. Let me out now!"

In three steps he reached her and did what came naturally. He turned her around and into his arms. She stiffened, struggling against him, but he held on, softly murmuring her name.

"What's wrong, Chey? What scared you? You're okay. I'm here. You're okay. Do you hear me? You're okay." As she trembled against him, he kept on talking, hoping to break through the terror he felt emanating from her body. On pure gut instinct, he said, "You're safe, Cheyenne. No one will hurt you ever again. I promise. Never again."

The trembling continued but she stopped

122

resisting and went limp against him. He didn't know what else to do so he went on holding her and whispering reassurances and promises to keep her safe. All the while, his mind chanted a prayer for guidance.

Something really bad had happened. And something about this garage had triggered a memory so dreadful she'd gone to pieces before his eyes.

God, help me. Help her.

"You're safe, baby. You're okay." He didn't know what else to say, so he kept on talking and praying, stroking her hair and her back as he would have Zoey's.

After a couple of minutes, she sucked in a shaky breath and pulled away. Instantly, he missed her, missed the way she'd curved into him as if made to fit there, missed the scent of her hair.

Averting her gaze, she crossed her arms protectively.

Still shaking, she licked her lips and whispered, "You must think I'm crazy."

He studied her stance, defensive but vulnerable. "No, but I think something's wrong. Talk to me, Cheyenne. I want to help."

She turned to the side, her profile tragic. "I don't like garages. Will you open the door, please? I have to get out of here."

He pressed the remote. The old door trembled

and groaned as it rose. As soon as the door cleared, she stepped out into the darkness. "I should go."

"Not until you talk to me."

She stared into the darkness. "I can't."

His gut clenched in disappointment. "Can't or won't?"

"Something happened a long time ago and I get claustrophobic."

"Claustrophobic?" Her terror had been far more than claustrophobia.

She rubbed her hands up and down her arms as if the temperature was freezing. "Yes. That's all. No big deal."

He didn't believe her. "Okay."

A beat passed while one lone tree frog croaked out a sad love song.

She started to walk away.

"Hey." She shouldn't leave this way, shaken and upset. "What about that popcorn?"

She turned back, indecision on her face. "I should go."

"Because of a little claustrophobia? Come on. Be a sport." Even though her car was still parked at the clinic only a short walk from his house, he'd worry about her all night if she left now.

"I can't. I'm sorry." With an expression that touched him to the marrow, she stalked away into the darkness.

Trace stood there, stunned and bewildered,

until her car started and the lights swung out onto Mercy Street and disappeared.

Raising his head to the sky, he whispered, "Okay, Lord, what just happened? And what do you expect me to do about it?"

Chapter Eight

C heyenne sat up most of the night thinking about the incident. She hadn't a flashback in months, but her therapist in Colorado Springs had warned her they could return without warning and continue for years.

But why now? And why in front of Trace, a man she actually respected and liked? A lot. He probably thought she was some kind of psycho.

Twice she opened her cell phone to call him but chickened out. Once she'd almost called her brother, but he wouldn't want to hear about it. Her flashbacks frightened him. Well, they scared her, too. Finally, she'd walked over to Kitty's pretty little cottage, but the lights were out. With a heart as heavy as a freight train, she'd gone back to her apartment and read the Bible Kitty kept in every room.

She'd wanted the words to help the way Trace

and Kitty claimed they would. They hadn't, but interestingly enough, she'd fallen asleep while reading. If that was all the Bible was good for, she'd take it. A few hours of peaceful sleep was a rare gift.

By the time she walked into the clinic the next morning, carrying two dozen doughnuts from the Sugar Shack, she was prepared to be fired. She'd say her goodbyes, check out of the motel and drive south until she ran out of gas.

A sick feeling gripped her belly. She didn't want to leave Redemption.

As she turned down the clinic hallway, Trace stepped out of an exam room, drying his hands on a paper towel. He spotted her and stopped dead still.

Her heart lurched. Here was another reason she didn't want to leave.

"Good morning," Trace said, his voice gravelly as though he hadn't slept well either.

"About last night—" she started.

He raised a palm. "Are you all right?"

The question melted her. He should be annoyed at her bizarre behavior and instead he expressed concern. How did she protect her battered heart against a man like that?

"Other than feeling stupid and embarrassed, I'm okay."

Tired blue eyes scoured her face. "Did I do something? Was it my fault?"

"No! Trace, no." The bakery bags whispered like dry leaves as she took another step forward. She was sorely tempted to touch him in reassurance, a temptation that both stunned and pleased her. "The problem is me. I'm—" She'd wondered all night what excuse would be enough. "I really am claustrophobic about closed garages. I freaked out." An understatement. "You couldn't have known."

The reply sounded reasonable. She hoped he'd buy it. He didn't. A man as intelligent and tuned in to people and animals as Trace would look deeper.

"What happened in Colorado, Cheyenne? What are you hiding from?"

Before she could formulate a half-truth reply, Toby ambled in the side door that led out to the kennels. The serious undercurrents were lost on him. With his usual happy demeanor, he said hello, then shuffled on past and into the store-room for cleaning supplies. As soon as Toby was out of sight, Trace took Cheyenne's arm and tugged her into the exam room he'd just come out of.

"I'm your friend. I want to help."

"I know. Your understanding means a lot to me."

"But you don't want to talk about Colorado."

The poor man had no idea what he was asking. If she told him the truth, he'd get that look, the one she'd seen too many times, the look that spoke sympathy and horror and, ultimately, withdrawal. No one wanted to be around her after they knew.

"I had some bad experiences, okay?" One really, really bad experience.

"Does this have anything to do with a guy?"

Cheyenne could feel the color draining from her skin. A man's evil leer flashed through her head.

"A boyfriend, I mean? Is there some guy waiting back in the Rockies who I should be worrying about?"

Worrying about? What did he mean by that?

"No, no guy. Not anymore."

"But there was?"

"I was engaged. He's marrying someone else." The admission came without the usual stab of hurt and betrayal.

Sympathetic understanding flared in Trace's eyes. "So that's the problem. He broke your heart and you ran away."

That was only part of the issue, but if knowing about Paul satisfied Trace's curiosity, Cheyenne didn't care what he believed. "I'm over him."

Maybe she really was. Maybe she'd never loved Paul in the first place. She'd certainly never really known him.

Trace propped a hip on the exam table and crossed his arms. "I'm glad."

"So I'm not fired?"

"Do you want to be?"

"No." She held up the white bakery bags. "I brought doughnuts as peace offerings."

"Maple?"

"And chocolate. With sprinkles."

That full-out, dimple-activating grin wreathed his face. "I made coffee an hour ago. It's probably sludge by now. Want some?"

She grinned back, relieved beyond words. If he thought she was crazy, he wasn't letting her know.

"Sludge is good after a sleepless night."

"You, too, huh?" He led the way to the cluttered room they all used for the rare moments of relaxation. A sink, a small table, a few metal cabinets, a refrigerator and a low counter were crammed with odds and ends. He went to the coffeepot and poured two cups.

"Straight up?" he asked.

"Hot and strong and blacker than midnight."

"Ah, a woman after my own heart."

The phrase was used all the time, so she tried not to read anything into the words, but a thin glow of pleasure went down with the first scalding sip of sludge. Before she realized what she was saying, she asked, "Could I get a rain check on that chili-cheese popcorn?"

Trace, his cup halfway to his lips, paused. "Seriously?"

She owed him. That was all. And she needed to prove to them both that she could go to his house without freaking out.

The house she could deal with. The garage was another matter.

"No woman can resist a bachelor's secret recipe for popcorn." She tried to keep the words light but they were partly true. At least, the part about not being able to resist a certain bachelor.

"Then you're on, tough girl." He pointed a finger at her nose. "Tonight."

"Tough girl?" Her lips curved above the cup.

He looked abashed. "That's the way I think of you. That chip on your shoulder. Your attitude. Tough girl."

"I wasn't so tough last night."

"Last night is forgotten. Today is the best day ever." Trace quoted the plaque hanging over the reception desk.

"No use wasting it."

He was definitely a Pollyanna. An irresistible quality, though Cheyenne figured she *was* crazy for spending any more time with him than her job required, but she had come to Redemption to start fresh. Might as well start tonight.

"Well, here we are, home sweet home." Trace pushed the front door open and let Cheyenne enter before him. The sleeve of her jacket brushed his arm, making her too aware of him again.

He had a powerful effect on her, and she was certainly old enough to recognize the signs. Attraction.

With Trace at her side, she entered the foyer that opened into the living room, a cozy space with a white fireplace and rust-colored furniture. A console piano gleamed with polish near a pair of sheer-draped windows.

"Your house is pretty," she said.

"My mom gets credit for that," he said.

As they approached the interior, Zoey, seated cross-legged at a low table, titled her head. "Who's with you, Daddy? Cheyenne?"

"How did you know?"

Zoey shrugged. "I can just tell."

"She has radar," Trace said, with a grin. "We figure she picks up sound and spatial clues—probably scent, too—but I'm still baffled when she does it."

A computer, earphones and an array of books and other school items were strewn around the second-grader. Two familiar-looking black puppies played at her side.

"I see you talked your dad into bringing Frog and Toad home with you." Cheyenne bent down to rub the silky fur.

"I'm the socializer. Playing with them makes them easier to adopt."

"And you love your job." Trace scrubbed his knuckles over the top of her head. "Admit it."

Zoey tilted her face upward. "Yeah. I love puppies. And kitties. And lambs."

"And any other living creature."

"Yes."

"Where's Grandma?" he asked, looking around as if he expected the woman to pop out of the woodwork.

"Right here, son." A round-figured woman with neatly coiffed sun-kissed hair and Trace's blue eyes entered from the far end of the living room. She shot a curious but friendly glance at Cheyenne.

"I'm Zoey's grandmother, Janie Bowman."

"I'm Cheyenne Rhodes. It's a pleasure to meet you. What is that amazing smell?"

"Mexican casserole." Janie patted her hip bones. "Loaded with fat and calories but you can afford it. I hope you're staying for dinner."

Trace looped an arm around his mother's shoulders. "That's the plan. Thanks, Mom."

She patted his cheek, an action Cheyenne found amusing. Trace was such a man, but to his mother he was still a boy.

"Gotta run, darlin'. The casserole is ready in the oven whenever you want to eat. Dad and I have dance class tonight."

"Knock 'em dead."

Janie Bowman kissed Zoey on the cheek and breezed out the door with a backward wave.

"She seems really nice."

"Mom's the best. I couldn't have survived without her help. She and Dad—" He stopped and shook his head. "They're awesome. When I bought the animal clinic, they sold their place near Tulsa and moved here, too. According to them, they wanted to retire to a quiet, friendly little town where Dad could garden and Mom could be more involved in the community."

"Do they do those things?"

"Oh, sure, but Zoey and I are the real reasons they came."

"You're lucky."

"Blessed. What about you?" he asked, crossing muscled forearms over his chest. "You have family somewhere?"

"Mom died when I was seventeen, but my dad and brother, Brent, still live in Colorado."

"Miss them?"

"A lot."

The unspoken question was on his face. Why wasn't she with them? But Trace was kind enough not to push.

Instead he turned his attention to his daughter. "So, how is the homework coming, Zoey girl?"

"Okay. I have to do this math paper, but I don't get it."

"What's not to get?" He went down on his haunches beside her, their shoulders touching, and ran his fingers over the page. There was no print, only raised bumps.

"You read Braille?" Cheyenne came to stand behind them, tempted to rest a hand on his shoulder. She didn't, of course.

"Have to. We both started learning when Zoey was about three, but Punkin-head here learned faster than I did. Her fingers fly. Mine still have to think about what I'm reading."

"Oh, Daddy, fingers can't think." Zoey lifted her face. "He always says silly things like that."

Cheyenne responded with a smile and then remembered that Zoey wouldn't know. The little girl was so well adapted that she often forgot.

"Three years old? I'm impressed. Do you attend regular school? I don't know how that works."

"Regular school," Trace said. "She has a classroom aid, but the goal is for her to be self-functioning with modifications by next year."

"Isn't that expecting a lot?"

"The world is sighted. She has to learn to live in it."

"She seems incredibly well adjusted to me already."

"Ah, she's all right." Trace pulled Zoey against him and kissed her forehead, pride in his touch and face. "For a punkin-head."

The little girl glowed with pleasure. "You're okay, too, for a silly monkey."

"So what's the problem with math?"

The telephone jangled. Zoey bolted up and grabbed the receiver.

"Dr. Bowman's residence," she said. Then her shoulders slouched. Apparently, the caller was not who she'd hoped. She held out the receiver. "For you, Daddy."

Trace took the phone and began to talk. Cheyenne immediately surmised that the caller was a patient. When he hung up, Trace confirmed her suspicions.

"I have to run out to Greg Teague's place and look at a cow. Want to ride along?"

"Daddy," Zoey said. "Please no. I have homework to finish and teacher said I should practice my keyboard. I don't want to go."

"You have to, Zoey. Grandma has plans tonight."

Without argument, Zoey started to gather her things. She'd been through this hundreds of times.

"I can stay here with Zoey," Cheyenne offered, feeling bad for the little girl. "You go on and take care of your patient."

Zoey clasped her hands in front of her and hopped up and down. "Will you really, Cheyenne? I'd love that. Say yes, Daddy. Please! Cheyenne can stay with me."

Trace swung his gaze to Cheyenne. "You serious?"

"Sure. We'll have fun. We'll play with the puppies and talk girl talk and maybe even play some games. Helping with math is out, though. I'm not as smart as Zoey. I can't read Braille."

"Zoey can handle the homework until I get back." Trace was already donning his jacket. "Go ahead and eat, too. There's no way of knowing how long I'll be gone." He paused at the door. "Are you sure about this, Cheyenne?"

Was he worried that she'd freak out again? "Go, Trace. Zoey and I will be fine. I promise."

"You have my cell number. Call if you need me."

He trusted her with his child. The pleasure surging through Cheyenne was all out of proportion to the event.

Even after she'd gone psycho in his garage, Trace still accepted and trusted her.

Trace heard the rich, happy notes of piano music the moment he shut off the truck engine. He hopped out of the cab and popped the locks, then stood in the darkened garage listening.

His mind flashed to Pamela. She had played like an angel and had dreamed of playing professionally until he'd come into her life. She'd loved the old Steinway, and even after her death Trace had retained the instrument for Zoey. No one had played that piano in years.

But someone was playing it now.

He pushed through the back door and into the

kitchen where the warm, spicy scent of Mom's casserole set his belly to growling. He was starved. But first, he wanted to let the ladies know he'd returned earlier than he'd dared hope.

The music covered his entrance and he stopped in the doorway between the dining and living room. His heart bumped hard at the sight before him. Their backs turned, black hair flowing, the pair could have been mother and daughter. On the floor at their feet, two pups sprawled in sleep, undisturbed by the piano.

He stepped up by the piano bench, and Cheyenne stopped playing. "You're back."

Before he could explain, Zoey whipped around, her face alight. "Daddy, I'm learning the piano. Just like Mommy. Cheyenne's teaching me. Aren't you, Cheyenne?"

Cheyenne stroked Zoey's hair. "If your dad agrees."

Trace got a funny lump in his throat. "No way I'd turn down an offer like that."

Cheyenne, still seated at an angle on the bench, smiled gently at his daughter. "She's an apt pupil. Very impressive."

"Yes, I'm impressive, Daddy. Cheyenne said. Let me show you." Zoey felt along the keys, placing her fingers just so. "Is this right, Cheyenne?"

"Play the notes and see if they sound right to you."

"Oh. Okay." Starting with the thumb, Zoey

137

played one note at a time, calling out each name, until she'd completed a scale. "I did it. I did it! Daddy, did you see me? Did you hear me? I know the keys now. Cheyenne showed me."

"All this in a little over an hour? I can't imagine what would happen if I left the two of you alone for an entire day."

"Cheyenne said next time I'll learn a whole song. Won't I, Cheyenne?"

Cheyenne, Cheyenne, Cheyenne. His daughter was clearly enamored of her new friend.

"I didn't know you played piano," he said to Cheyenne.

She shrugged as though her considerable skill were no big deal. "My family is musical. Everyone plays something. I took lessons from age four until I became a rebellious teenager."

"Zoey's mother played."

"Zoey told me. You don't play?"

"I wish, but these fingers only know how to doctor animals."

"Nothing wrong with that. Especially when you're as good with animals as you are." Her simple little compliment made his head spin. "Is Greg Teague's cow okay? You're back sooner than we expected."

"Old cow with a new calf. Greg thought she might have a prolapsed uterus, but she didn't. After an exam and a little conversation, I was out of there."

138

"I'm glad."

She was? Well, so was he, and no, he wasn't ready to name the glow of pleasure beneath his collarbone.

"Thanks for letting me stay with Zoey."

He frowned. "Why wouldn't I?"

One shoulder came up in a feminine shrug. "After last night . . ."

He'd never considered worrying about Zoey with Cheyenne. Maybe he should, but not for the reason she thought. "The past is forgotten. Remember?"

She laughed. "Forgotten. Remember. Is that double talk? Or are you trying to confuse me?"

He grinned. "I like hearing you laugh."

Looking flustered, she pushed a lock of hair behind one ear. "You must be hungry."

The comment sounded wifely. Trace nipped that very dangerous thought in the bud faster than he could say penicillin.

"Starved." That was why he was anxious to get home. Food. Not a certain mysterious woman whose laugh had his stomach doing acrobatics.

Cheyenne patted Zoey's hand and pushed off the bench, taking care not to step on Frog and Toad. "Go ahead and play if you want, Zoey. Your dad needs to eat dinner."

"I can fix my own. No problem," he said.

She gave him an appraising glance and went right on into the kitchen to dish up dinner. He followed after her like a grateful pup, willing his eyes not to watch her walk and his brain not to enjoy the bounce of her hair.

"Your mother is a great cook," she was saying. "This stuff is incredible." She set the tantalizing dish on the table, steaming hot. "Want some salad? Zoey and I made one."

"Sure. I'll get it, though. You're my guest."

"I don't mind. Sit down. You look exhausted."

"Sweet-talker." But he scraped a chair away from the round table and sat, grateful to relax, while Cheyenne moved around his kitchen as though she'd been here dozens of times.

How long had passed since a woman other than his mother had served him dinner? Margo had been here on occasion, but he'd done the cooking and serving. Margo had always been a guest. With Cheyenne—well, Cheyenne seemed to belong.

He grabbed for the glass of ice water and gulped, washing down the aberrant thinking. What was the matter with him to think such a thing? Last night, Cheyenne had bolted out of his garage like a startled deer. Just because she and Zoey got on well was no reason for him to start thinking crazy thoughts.

His belly clutched at the realization. His little girl was forming a powerful attachment to Cheyenne. At the clinic, Zoey wanted Cheyenne's attention every minute. She talked about her at home, too. And now, tonight, she'd wanted to be with Cheyenne instead of him.

This was not good. She could get hurt.

Face it, Doc, a small voice whispered. *You could get hurt, too.*

Cheyenne was touchy and unpredictable, with plenty of pain lurking behind those beautiful dark eyes. Her protective wall might be too high to climb.

And where would that leave him and Zoey?

He'd best remember that she was his employee, one that baffled him much of the time. She was the needy one, not him. God had sent her along for him to help, not fall for.

Crazy as it sounded, he feared he could fall for her very easily.

Sometimes the heart of a man made no sense at all.

He'd spent a year wishing he could fall in love with Margo and finally coming to the realization that she was a friend and could never be anything else. She was a good woman, wife material, and kind to his daughter. He should have been able to love her. Yet he couldn't.

Then Cheyenne stormed into his life with a box of puppies, a chip on her shoulder and sorrow in her eyes, and he couldn't think of anyone but her.

He scooped a man-size helping of cheesy casserole onto his plate and shoved it around with a fork.

Maybe that was the problem. Maybe his over-active sense of Good Samaritan had kicked into high gear.

But he didn't think so. The feelings stirring inside him did not qualify as compassion.

He cast a furtive glance at the troublesome woman. She was at the refrigerator, her back to him, long, glossy hair tumbling around her shoulders. She turned suddenly, salad bowl in hand, and caught him staring. He quickly looked down at his plate, as uncomfortable as a blushing, bumbling teenager.

Clearing his throat, he said, "Thanks for looking after Zoey tonight."

"No problem." She slid the fluted bowl of green salad in front of him along with a bottle of salad dressing and took the chair across from him. Seeing her there, arms folded on his table, leaning toward him with a tilt at the corners of her mouth, did strange things to his insides. "We had fun. She's a great little girl."

"Yeah. She is." He shoved a bite of cheesy casserole into his mouth.

Too great to have her heart broken.

But what could he do to stop it from happening?

Chapter Nine

~

This time she fought. No one would ever again say she hadn't fought hard enough, that she could have done more, that she could have avoided the attack.

Straining with all her strength, she shoved hard at his chest. He was so heavy. And terrifyingly stronger. Why didn't people understand that?

Her head made sharp contact with something metal as her attacker shoved her down into the car seat. Rough cloth and a protruding seat belt dug into the bare skin of her back.

The acrid taste of terror and her own blood pooled on her tongue.

The smell of him filled her nostrils. She struggled not to gag. For weeks, she couldn't wash away his smell.

She grabbled at her side for the Glock. Where was it? Where *was* it?

A knife pressed against her throat, cold and sharp. Her breath caught just behind the metal blade. She shoved at his arm, then sank her teeth into his flesh.

His fist slammed into the side of her head.

Gray sparks shot everywhere. Her arms went weak. Helpless.

Not again. Not again. Please, please, not again. Struggling to remain conscious, she thrashed her head from side to side, trying to escape. But there was no escape.

Sweat beaded on Dwight Hector's evil face and dripped into her wide, desperate eyes. He laughed.

She saw her own reflection in his mad irises and feared she was going to die.

Cheyenne screamed. The sound echoed in her head, and went on and on and on.

With a jolt, she awakened and sat upright, panting. Her heart pounded hard enough to break a rib.

Another scream came and then a whimper.

Though her body quaked from the nightmare, she dragged both hands over her sweating face and tried to awaken. The lights were on, as they always were. She couldn't sleep without light anymore. The counselor called the behavior a coping skill. She called it psychotic, but she left them on just the same.

The scream came again. A muffled, short cry.

Cheyenne was fully awake now, but the remnants of the nightmare toyed with her sanity.

Someone was screaming and it wasn't her. A woman. In the unit next to hers.

Reaching beneath the cool pillow, she closed

her shaky fingers around the cold, comforting steel of the baby Glock.

Pushing away the covers, she tiptoed to the wall and leaned an ear to listen. Pleading moans came from the other room. Whimpers. A woman's voice raised in desperation.

The cop in her reacted.

In three minutes flat, she had tugged clothes over her pajamas and was banging on the door of Unit 5.

"Hello, hello!" she called. "Open the door." She almost said, "Police," but caught herself in time.

A curse followed by a flurry of movement went on inside the unit. When heavy footsteps came closer, Cheyenne concealed the pistol behind her back and stepped slightly to the side, ready for whatever and whoever opened that door.

The door opened a crack. Light seeped out. A man's face appeared. A familiar face. The man who stomped a Yorkie and abused his wife. Ray Madden.

Even in the blocked lighting, his eyes were bloodshot, but a glimmer of recognition flashed through them. "What do you want?"

Alcohol breath assailed her.

"I'm in the next unit." Cheyenne surreptitiously slid the toe of her boot into the opening. "Does someone in here need help?"

"No."

But Cheyenne saw his sneer and the way his

gaze slid to the side as though someone was behind him. She wasn't leaving until she saw Emma. "I heard a scream."

"Bad dream." He raked a hand over the top of disheveled blond hair. When his arm came up, Cheyenne caught a glimpse of the small woman huddled on the bed behind him.

"Are you alone?" She leaned to peer around him.

He shifted to block her view. "You offering company?"

She was running out of patience. "Look, we both know your wife is in here and I'm not leaving until I talk to her."

"This is a private family matter. You should mind your own business."

Ignoring the hulking man, she called out, "Emma, I'm here to help. You don't have to stay here. You can come with me right now and I'll see that you're safe."

"She don't need anybody's help."

"Let *her* tell me that." She shoved her boot a little farther inside, giving the door a push.

"You could get hurt busting in here." The man's voice was a low growl of warning.

Using her iciest cop stare and a voice that said she was in charge, even though she felt as weak as a cooked noodle, she demanded, "Let her talk to me. *Now.*"

A string of bourbon-soaked expletives dirtied

the air, but the man relented. Opening the door, he pivoted toward the pale woman. "Get over here, stupid. Nosy witch won't leave until you do. Tell her to get lost. To mind her own business if she knows what's good for her."

Emma was crying, one hand over her mouth to stifle the noise. Her white blouse was spotted with blood, probably from the bleeding nose and mouth.

Fury rippled through Cheyenne. She was sorely tempted to stick the Glock in this buzzard's face.

Instead, she kept her voice soothing. "Do you need help?"

Head down, the cowed woman moved across the beige carpeting on shaky legs.

"No," she whispered, but even in the dim lighting, her bruises told a different tale. "I'm okay."

Sure she was. And pigs flew. A two-hundred-fifty-pound man with fists like hams beating up on a wife half his size did not make her okay. Cheyenne had witnessed this scenario plenty of times, but nowadays she took it personally.

"You heard her," the dirtbag said. "She's fine. Now get lost." He started to close the door. Cheyenne braced an arm across it.

"You don't have to stay here and be abused. I'll help you. Just walk out right now. Come with me."

Temptation flickered in the woman's face but was quickly extinguished when her husband placed his hand on the back of her neck.

"Me and Emma just had a little lovers' spat and now I've come to take her home and make up. She knows I can't live without her." His fingers tightened on the woman's neck. She flinched but didn't try to escape. "Isn't that right, baby?"

Cheyenne kept her attention on the woman, willing her to listen, to escape while she could. "Emma, this has happened before, hasn't it? He hurt your dog, too."

Emma answered with a rapid blink of red-rimmed eyes, but only said, "Ray, he gets a little jealous when he's drinking. I'm all right. He didn't mean anything by it."

"You can come with me. I'll see that you're safe."

"You heard her, lady. Back off."

"I'm not leaving until *she* says so."

His nostrils flared in fury. His jaw clenched and he leaned toward Cheyenne, menacing. "Beat it!"

She braced herself, glaring back, warning him.

The fingers of her right hand, still behind her back, slid into position on the pistol.

Give me a reason, you dirtbag.

Like most bullies, he must have seen the steel in Cheyenne's manner and understood that she would not back down. He changed tactics.

"Well, if you ain't leaving, we are. Get your stuff, baby." He gave a not-too-gentle thrust that sent Emma scurrying toward a backpack on the foot of the bed. "We're going home."

Though her nose still dripped blood, Emma followed her husband's orders. While Cheyenne watched in sad silence, the trembling woman tossed a few things into the backpack and sat down on the end of the bed, hands twisting in her lap. She refused to meet Cheyenne's probing gaze.

"I guess that answers your questions, lady. Emma is my wife. She stays with me. Till death do us part." His mouth curved in an ugly smile.

Every one of them recognized his last words as a threat, but unless Emma wanted help, Cheyenne could do nothing.

"Are you sure, Emma?" Cheyenne asked one more time.

Eyes downcast, Emma nodded.

Cheyenne had seen domestic violence dozens of times and though she'd studied the psychology of abuse, she could never understand why women refused help. Still, most times they did. All she could do was offer hope.

"If you should change your mind, I'm next door. And I will get you help and keep you safe. You have my word."

Emma's soft thank-you was nearly lost as the door slammed in Cheyenne's face.

149

•••

Shaking all over, Cheyenne dropped the pistol hand to her side and leaned the back of her head against the exterior wall. The siding was slick and hard, the night air cool. She took a deep, shuddering breath, barely able to remain upright now that the danger was over. Adrenaline jacked through her system like rocket fuel.

What had she been thinking to accost this perp single-handedly with no backup? She hadn't been thinking at all. She'd been dreaming.

The doorknob rattled as if the guests in Unit 5 were coming out. Security lights glowed above each unit, making her far too visible. She edged behind a squat evergreen and crouched low, out of sight, pistol resting on her thigh.

She mustered all her inner determination not to sink to the ground, roll into a ball and let the terror sweep over her in waves the way it had before.

The door opened. She slowed her breathing to match the quiet night.

The man and woman came out. The oversize creep had his arm around Emma. As if he knew Cheyenne was watching, he stopped beneath the light, tilted his wife's chin and kissed her, long and deep.

Cheyenne nearly gagged. Emma simply submitted.

"You know I love you, baby," he said.

Emma nodded, then dropped her head and followed her husband to a car. She opened her own door and got inside. And they roared away into the darkness.

If she thought it would do any good, Cheyenne would have said a prayer for the very young woman.

As the engine noise slowly faded and quiet night sounds returned, cold sweat popped out on Cheyenne's face and neck.

She dragged in more fresh air. Green grass. Cedar. The lingering smell of alcohol.

Stomach roiling, she bent forward, rested her hands on her thighs and threw up.

Ray Madden had reminded her too much of Dwight Hector. Her fingers had itched to shoot his leering face. She'd wanted to.

When the sick spasm ended, she raked a shaky sleeve across her mouth.

What kind of person had she become?

"Cheyenne? Is that you?"

The voice, coming out of the dark night and on the tail of the incident, shot electricity through Cheyenne's bloodstream. She spun, both hands on the weapon, ready.

On the narrow pathway between the parking lot and the cedar bushes, Kitty Wainright froze. Beneath the unnatural security lighting, her face turned as white as her flowing robe. "You have a gun."

At the quivery, stunned words, Cheyenne slid the pistol into the back of her jeans. "Sorry. Didn't mean to scare you."

Mule slippers scraped against the white gravel as Kitty stepped closer, her expression a jumble of emotions. She must have rushed out, tossing the robe on as she moved. The soft yellow chenille hung open over pale-colored capri pajamas. Her usually upswept hair hung loose and long, surprisingly to her waist. She looked like a modern-day Rapunzcl.

"I heard a noise, and then saw a car drive away as if someone was chasing it. Who was that? What happened? Is Emma all right?"

Calmer now, though her insides were still raw and acidic, Cheyenne related the story in her best dispatched manner.

Kitty wasn't as calm. "Cheyenne! You could have been hurt. Why didn't you call the police?"

"I *am* the pol—" She stopped, but it was too late.

Kitty's eyes widened. She crossed her arms, shivering a little. "You're a cop?"

Cheyenne squeezed her eyelids tight. Now she'd done it. "Was."

A silence ensued. She could practically hear the questions flying around inside Kitty's head. Questions she did not want to answer.

Kitty touched her arm. "You look shaken. I think we could both use a cup of tea."

A year ago, Cheyenne would have requested tequila—straight up—but she'd learned the lesson of sobriety the hard way. Tonight, she was glad for the offer of tea.

In minutes, she was seated in Kitty's kitchen, a room every bit as breezy and cheerful as its decorator, but the rattling in her bones continued. She couldn't get the battered Emma off her mind.

She knew how a woman felt to be helpless and scared and at the mercy of a stronger, meaner opponent. Propping an elbow on Kitty's pretty glass table, she leaned her head on the heel of her hand and closed her eyes.

The ugly scene played out again with a familiar refrain. Could she have done anything differently?

Cheyenne sighed in futility and sat back, forcing her attention to anything except the visions in her head. She'd not sleep another minute tonight.

The pilot igniter made a click-clicking sound as Kitty turned on the gas and plunked a red teakettle on to heat. She opened a glass-fronted cabinet, took down two shiny red mugs with matching saucers and set them on the table. Her long, sun-blond hair swung and swayed as she moved around the small space.

With upraised brows, she lifted a little pink

and green basket filled with a variety of bagged teas. "Peppermint might ease your stomach."

Kitty had seen her puking her guts up. Lovely. "Peppermint's fine."

"I have coffee if you'd rather."

"Tea is better. Thanks." She was already so hyped up she could thread a running sewing machine. Coffee was the last thing she needed.

Kitty finished the preparations and placed the two cups, milk and sugar on the table before sitting down.

"I suspected this was the reason Emma's been coming here," she said, elbows on the table, cup lifted halfway to her lips.

"Tonight isn't the first time?"

Kitty shook her head. "No. Well, yes. This is the first time anything bad has happened, but she's spent the night in one of my units three or four times. She usually arrives late or on Saturday evening."

Cheyenne's teeth clenched. "Whenever he gets drunk and mean. I knew something bad was going on with them." She told Kitty about the incident at the clinic. "I suspected abuse that day. So did Trace."

"Terrible." Kitty blew daintily over the top of her tea. A curl of steam rose and circled her nose. "I've noticed the bruises, old ones and new ones on her arms. Sometimes on her face, too. I figured she comes here to hide from him, but when I've tried to talk to her about it, she shuts me out. Then she checks out early the next morning before I can try again. This is the first time her husband's found her, though."

Cheyenne's lip curled. "The dirtbag."

A small twitch of humor lifted Kitty's lips. "You sound like a cop when you say that."

"Even when I was a police officer, my hands were tied unless the victim wanted help." She dumped two spoonfuls of sugar into the hot tea and stirred. The peppermint scent rose up, soothing. "That's what frustrates me most about domestic violence. Until she asks for help or he kills her, there's nothing we can do."

"We can pray."

Yeah, well, she wasn't holding her breath on that one.

Kitty set her cup aside and casually asked, "Want to talk about why you're not a cop anymore? Redemption can always use another good police officer."

"I don't see myself going back to law enforcement."

"What happened? And don't say nothing, because I've known from the first day you walked in the office that something bad had happened."

"Everyone has problems."

"True, but not everyone leaves a career and moves across the country because of them."

Cheyenne clinked the red cup into the saucer and pushed back from the table. "I really should go. You need to get some sleep."

Kitty placed a forestalling hand atop hers. "Finish your tea. I promise to hush my mouth."

Cheyenne eased back in place. "Sorry. I don't mean to be touchy. You've been wonderful to me, but Colorado was a bad time."

"I understand about bad times, Cheyenne. You'll be surprised to find a lot of kindred spirits here in Redemption."

"Oh, yeah, I forgot," she said, trying to lighten the heavy topic. "Redemption is some kind of magical magnetic force field for damaged souls."

Kitty laughed softly. "Magic has nothing to do with Redemption. Have you seen the well at Town Square?"

Cheyenne didn't understand what some nineteenth-century well had to do with anything, particularly her. She was practically a stranger in Redemption. "I've seen it, but I don't get the significance."

"Give yourself time. You will."

The cryptic statement didn't help at all.

"Trace took me there, and I felt as if he was disappointed because I didn't have a big revelation from God or something."

Kitty paused, one hand over her teacup. "Trace took you to see the well?"

Cheyenne glanced away, uncomfortable with the speculation in Kitty's eyes. "He and Zoey were showing the new girl around. No big deal."

"Burgers at Big Bob's, late nights at the clinic, supper at Trace's house." She dipped a tea bag up and down in the cup of steaming water. "I think something's going on with the two of you."

Cheyenne's heart bumped. "How could you possibly know all that?"

Kitty's merry laugh rang out. "Redemption is a small town, and Trace is a single, attractive businessman. Anything our good doctor does is noticed. People like him."

"They should. Half of them never get charged a dime."

"And I can guess which ones. The older folks on fixed incomes. The single mothers whose kids love their pets but can't afford vet bills. Trace cares about people as well as animals, Cheyenne."

Trace cared about everyone, not just her. She was his latest project, his employee. That was all.

She should feel good about that. She didn't.

After tonight's unexpected battle with a drunk, abusive husband, her emotions were in a worse jumble than ever. With all the garbage piled up inside her, she was scared to examine her feelings for Trace Bowman lest she open a Pandora's box she couldn't handle.

"He's a good guy."

"A very good guy with a special child to consider. I wouldn't want to see either of them hurt."

Cheyenne's stomach tightened. Kitty's warning was laughable. Several women "dropped by" the clinic on a regular basis, including Margo, the woman Trace had been dating. He couldn't be attracted to a messed-up former cop.

Yet some indefinable emotion buzzed between the two of them every time they were in the same building. Whether alone or with patients and staff around them, she knew where Trace was all the time. When she glanced his way, his twinkling gaze met hers.

And Zoey—darling Zoey—touched a maternal spot she hadn't known existed. Concern for the little girl was one very good reason not to fall for the father. Zoey deserved better.

"Neither would I," she said finally. She would leave town before causing hurt to either of them.

Depression crept over her like a dark cloud—a cloud that had followed her from Colorado Springs to Redemption, Oklahoma.

"Can we talk about something else?" she asked, and heard the despair in her tone.

Kitty's guileless blue eyes seemed to look deep inside her. "Anything you choose, Cheyenne. I want to help, not make things worse."

"You have. You are. I appreciate your friendship more than I can tell you."

"Enough to come to Bible study?"

Cheyenne gave a short laugh. "I'll think about it."

"Good enough." Silky hair swinging, Kitty pushed back from the table. "I need a cookie. How about you?"

"Sure." She watched while Kitty opened a whimsical kitten cookie jar and returned with a half dozen chocolate chip cookies. "Cute cookie jar."

"Mmm-hmm. I like it. Jace bought it for me."

"Jace? Is this your guy?"

As if startled at the suggestion, Kitty shook her head. "Jace Carter is a good friend and the best building contractor in Redemption. He does all the upkeep on the motel."

"And he buys you kitty cookie jars? Sounds like a very interested friend to me."

A powerful sadness shifted over Kitty's usually upbeat countenance. "I was loved by Dave Wainright. No one can ever top that."

Silence hung over the scented tea and cookies. Though normally averse to prying, Cheyenne had to know. "Tell me about Dave."

"He was my one true love. Strong and funny and full of God." A sad smile lifted the corners of her bow mouth. "I can't remember a moment of unhappiness in our two-year marriage. Every day I woke up beside him was a gift of joy. He never went to sleep before I did. You know why?"

"Why?"

"Because he said he didn't want to miss one moment of our time together." Graceful fingers fiddled with the tea-bag string. "He would prop up on his elbow and smile down at me until I fell asleep."

"What happened?"

"He went to war. Not much else to say."

The overdose of patriotic memorabilia suddenly made sense. "I'm sorry."

"Me, too. Oh, me, too." Kitty's blue eyes grew glassy. "You want more tea?"

"I should go." Cheyenne glanced at the clock above Kitty's stove. The timepiece matched the kitten cookie jar. "Morning will be here soon."

But neither made a move.

"I don't think I can sleep," Kitty said. "Can you?"

Cheyenne wondered what Kitty would say if she told her how little she'd slept in the past year. "Not much hope."

"I notice your lights stay on really late."

"Insomnia," she said, though more than the inability to sleep kept the lights burning. Fear, as much as she hated to give in to the emotion, gathered like buzzards after dark. If she turned off the lights, they flapped around her bed as they'd done that night in Trace's garage, threatening to pluck her heart out.

"I had trouble sleeping after Dave died."

"What did you do?"

"I cried a lot." Kitty's lips curved in self-mockery. "Friends here in Redemption helped. And I prayed. Oh, how I prayed."

"Weren't you the least bit ticked off at God?"

"Absolutely! I told Him about it, too. There were days I'd drive out to the river where no one could hear me and I'd yell at Him. I'd demand to know why the best man I ever knew had to die and I'd pray to die, too. Sometimes I'd lie down and beat the ground with my fists."

The admission both surprised and saddened Cheyenne. Calm, cheery Kitty was not the screaming, pounding type. Her agony must have been overwhelming.

"Did it help?"

"Gradually. Pain that deep doesn't heal in an instant, Cheyenne. But God tenderly let me take out my grief on Him. I could feel Him all around me, loving me even when I was so terribly angry."

The comment gave Cheyenne food for thought. She wasn't angry, though. She was wrecked, a jumble of painful emotions that she couldn't always understand or control. She hated being weak, hated being out of control. Guilt and shame and depression warred with common sense and the need to move past that awful day last year. Could God fix that? Trace said He could. And now Kitty.

161

She closed her eyes and breathed in. Oh, how she wished the words were true.

As if Kitty could read her thoughts, she lightly touched Cheyenne's wrist. "When you're ready to talk about whatever happened, I'm a very good listener. And I know how to keep my mouth shut. You can count on that. And I can pray." She lifted slender shoulders in a graceful shrug. "I'll pray anyway. God knows what's bothering you even if I don't. And He cares, sweetie. He really cares."

A lump formed in Cheyenne's throat.

Oh, God, if it were only true.

Chapter Ten

Trace's boots made a hollow echo as he stepped up onto the old wooden porch. He lifted the knocker, a bizarre apparatus made from a shoe heel. A wire snaked from the heel through a tiny hole in the door. He knew from experience what would happen the moment he knocked.

He struck the heel against the lopsided door, a salvaged castoff from somewhere, as were most of the items in the home of G. I. Jack and Popbottle Jones.

The *oogah* horn of a Model T Ford vibrated through the wall.

As if she'd been watching and waiting—and she may have been—a Nubian nanny goat came galloping around the corner, bleating her head off. Petunia was the best watchdog in town. No one sneaked by on her watch.

When she saw her vet, she put on the brakes, her slick hooves skidding over the wooden planks like skis on ice. Long ears flying out behind, she came to a slow, screeching halt six inches away.

Trace rubbed the hard skull with his knuckles. "Good morning, Petunia. Anybody home around here?"

Two dogs crawled from beneath the elevated porch and shook themselves, fluffing out thick, shaggy coats. The first, an enormous brindle mutt with short, half-cocked ears and a comical expression, took one look at the visitor, yelped and belly-crawled back under the porch.

Trace grinned. Apparently, Biscuit remembered his last trip to the clinic. "Sorry, buddy. No hard feelings."

The other dog, an odd-looking creature with short, stubby legs, a disproportionately long body and enough dirty white fur to be a sheep, held no grudges. The fat plume curled over his back flopped back and forth in greeting. He groveled toward Trace, his teeth showing in a doggy smile.

Trace went to a knee to ruffle the thick mane. "How ya doin', Gravy?"

Gravy flopped over for a belly rub. Petunia, disturbed by the dog's interference, butted Trace's shoulder as if to say, "I was here first."

Disentangling himself from the animals, Trace tried the knocker again. The old gentlemen were usually home this early in the day, having made their sunrise trek to the Sugar Shack for breakfast and the latest news.

Shading his eyes against the morning glare, Trace looked around the yard.

G. I. Jack and Popbottle Jones lived on the edge of town in a red-framed house that may have once been a barn. The outside was littered with the results of their avocation—Dumpster-diving. In the backyard, outbuildings and lean-tos housed even more of their discoveries and included a snug little barn for the animals. An old tractor, a hay baler that probably hadn't worked in thirty years and an ancient, rusty pickup with the hood lifted rounded out the landscape.

There was no sign of G.I. or Popbottle.

The *oogah,* however, activated the goat and Gravy. Gravy barked. Petunia bleated. The doorbell *oogahed.* Biscuit stayed in his hiding place.

"What's all the racket up here?"

Trace pivoted to the opposite side and saw G. I. Jack limping around the corner of the house, wiping his hands on an old towel. His ever-present

164

army cap was on backward and tufts of gray hair poked up around his ears. His camo jacket hung open to reveal a T-shirt announcing his donation to a recent blood drive. A small bag of red peanuts peeked from his chest pocket.

Both the dog and the goat abandoned Trace the moment their master appeared.

"Oh, it's you, Doc. How ya doin'?"

"Good. Yourself?"

"Tolerable. Tolerable." G.I.'s old head bobbed with each word. "Come on in the house. We'll find a cup of joe."

Trace followed the older man inside. Petunia tip-tapped in behind him.

Trace had visited the home enough not to be surprised by the disorder surrounding him. The two old gents collected anything and every-thing and found uses for most of it. Boxes and barrels held items for recycling—everything from the usual aluminum cans and plastics to ink cartridges and packing peanuts. In the center of a living room decorated with a hodgepodge of intriguing, often unidentifiable objects, a bicycle stood on its head, the wheelless body sticking up in the air. Of particular interest was a sculpture taking shape next to the woodstove.

"What's this?" Trace asked.

"Gonna be a horse. Maybe just the head, I'm thinking." G.I. removed his cap and scratched at the thatch of hair. "I never know until I'm done.

165

Stuff just kinda takes shape on its own."

With genuine interest, Trace studied the growing arrangement of metals and wires. Was that a hubcap he spotted? If he used his wildest imagination, he could make out the image of a horse. "Got a buyer yet?"

"That museum up in Minnesota's been calling. I think they might like this."

Newcomers were often surprised to discover the comical old veteran was a gifted artist and inventor who made a pretty fair living with his art by using nothing but junk for his creations. The chandelier hanging overhead was one such project, made of colored bottles and draped with discarded beads that refracted light in interesting, almost stained-glass patterns.

G.I. shuffled to a counter littered with spare parts and empty jars. "You needin' more of Petunia's milk?"

"That I am." Trace took the offered cup of coffee. "Can you spare a gallon or two?"

"Petunia's happy to share her milk, aren't you, darling girl?"

The nanny was too busy chewing on the vinyl tablecloth to notice.

"Now, you stop that. You've had breakfast." G.I. pushed the goat's head to one side. She bleated her annoyance but refrained from eating anything else.

"Sit down, Doc. Take a load off while I get that

milk. I got a hunk of Petunia's cheese, too. Think Zoey would like that?"

"I know she would." G.I. always had a little something for Zoey, be it a gadget he'd made or a chunk of cheese. "She's still driving me crazy with that whistle."

A few weeks ago, G.I. had presented Zoey with a whistle made from an empty shotgun shell. Neither Trace nor the kennel full of dogs had enjoyed the gift nearly as much as Zoey had.

G.I. chuckled. "How's she and Cheyenne getting on?"

The question caught Trace off guard. His pulse bumped against his collarbone. He'd done his best all morning not to think about Cheyenne, but she invaded his thoughts at every turn. "Cheyenne and Zoey?"

"Um-hmm. They getting along all right?"

The truth was Zoey had formed a fast attachment to Cheyenne. They'd bonded over piano, puppies and subtraction problems. This morning, Zoey was full of Cheyenne-isms.

Cheyenne brushed my hair. Cheyenne said I have beautiful blue eyes. Cheyenne took ballet when she was little. Can I take ballet?

All he said to G. I. Jack was, "Zoey likes everyone."

"That's our Zoey." G.I.'s grizzled head bobbed. "Child like her don't need eyes, 'cause she's got vision."

For a simple man of little education, G. I. Jack sometimes showed astounding wisdom.

"I guess you're right, G.I. Zoey's got a lot of love."

"Mmm-hmm. Sure does." The older man scrubbed his hands under the faucet and then took a cloth-wrapped package from the refrigerator. "How about you? You like her?"

"Zoey? Crazy about her."

G.I. guffawed. "You know who I mean."

Trace knew all right, but he wasn't ready to go there. "Cheyenne's a quick learner. She's becoming a great assistant in a hurry."

"Work ain't what I'm talking about."

"Work is what *I'm* talking about."

"Okay, okay." Chuckling, G.I. extracted a butcher knife from a drawer and sliced into the chunk of pale goat cheese. "Did you show her the well the other night?"

"I did. She didn't say anything." He'd hoped the Bible verse would generate some questions or get her to discuss what was bothering her. It hadn't.

"Well, healing takes time."

"You noticed, too?"

"Couldn't miss it. First day we seen her, me and Popbottle spotted trouble. We figured you and the Lord was what she needed to fix her right up."

Trace's heart dropped into his boots. Hadn't

168

he been thinking the same crazy thoughts? "Me?"

"Sure. You and Zoey. You said Zoey likes her. And we're figuring you do, too. We notice things, you know."

The two old dudes didn't miss a thing. If they started in on him, he was toast. His head swam with thoughts of Cheyenne constantly. The more he was with her, the closer he wanted to be. Now G.I. and Popbottle were noticing his distraction.

Dangerous. He was not only risking his own heart; he was risking Zoey's.

Zoey gravitated to any creature in need. From frightened, abused animals and the slow but gentle Toby to her overweight best friend from school, Zoey saw with her heart. And her heart saw something special in Cheyenne Rhodes.

His gut clenched. He did, too.

"I can promise you right smart that Cheyenne's taken with Zoey, too. Any woman would be."

"She offered to teach Zoey piano."

"You gonna let her?"

"Probably." He'd already agreed, but the sensible, protective part of his brain wanted to hold back.

"Might be good for the child to have a woman's attention."

"She's got my mom."

"A fine woman, your mother." The knife *whack-*

whacked against the kitchen counter. "Does your mother play piano?"

Trace's lips twisted. G. I. Jack would get his point across one way or the other. "I don't want Zoey hurt."

G.I. paused, the knife poised over the pale mound of cheese. "And you're thinking Cheyenne might walk."

"No." Trace steepled his fingers together and stared at them. "I think she might run. She's run away from Colorado. What's to say she won't keep moving?"

"I got this feeling." G.I. tapped his sternum with a backward-pointing thumb. The knifepoint nearly poked him in the chin.

"Cheyenne's only been here a short time and already Zoey's more attached to her than she ever was to Margo." Trace reached for his coffee cup.

"Maybe you are, too." G.I. returned to his work.

Trace swirled the remaining coffee round and round, staring at the blackness. His own reflection stared back. Was G.I. right? Had his original desire to minister to Cheyenne become something more personal?

He was afraid it had.

In defense, he said, "When did you take up matchmaking, G.I.?"

G. I. Jack chuckled. "Long time ago, and you know it."

The butcher knife slid through the cheese and thumped hard against the countertop. "Zoey needs a mama. You need a wife. Nothing wrong with friends giving you a little push in the right direction."

"Who's to say Cheyenne is the right direction? We barely know each other." Although last night, when he'd walked in on Cheyenne and Zoey, he'd felt as if he were coming home for the first time in years.

"I knew my Ethel three weeks before we married. We was happy as pigs in a mud wallow till the day she died. Forty-two years." The grizzled gray head bobbed. "Forty-two and not near long enough. How long you know each other don't matter, boy. Heart time and listening to the Lord's leading, that's what matters."

The old man had a point, but as much as Trace was drawn to Cheyenne, he was afraid, too. He'd loved before, deeply. Losing a love like that cut deeper that G.I.'s butcher knife. "I like the things I know about Cheyenne. It's the things I don't know that worry me."

"Does she ever talk about 'em?"

"No, but once . . ." He paused, hesitant to discuss that night in the garage. Cheyenne had a right to privacy.

G. I. Jack pointed the butcher knife at him. "Might as well tell me. Somebody will."

Few things in Redemption got past the sharp

171

eyes and ears of G. I. Jack and Popbottle Jones.

Trace sipped at the coffee, realizing that this, not the goat's milk, was the reason he'd come here. G. I. Jack and Popbottle Jones had been there for him when he'd first moved to Redemption. Their prayers and advice had helped set him on the right path.

"Just between us, all right?"

"Sure thing. Well, and maybe Popbottle. We're partners in prayer, remember."

Trace nodded. Though the two old gents knew everything in town and didn't mind sharing news, their word was golden. He'd shared secrets at this table before and never had one betrayed. "I invited her to the house one night after a call."

"For some of your mama's popcorn, I guess."

"My popcorn," he corrected, grinning. "Everything seemed normal. We got out of the truck and started inside and . . ." He paused, running a hand over the back of his neck. "I don't know how to explain what transpired. One minute she was fine and the next she was shaking and scared and wanted out of the garage."

G.I. put aside the knife, eyes narrowed in thought. "What did you do?"

"I tried to calm her down." He remembered how fragile and lovely she'd felt in his arms, and how holding her had made him feel like the biggest man on the planet. He'd never been all

172

that macho driven, but the tough girl brought out the protective male in him. "She said garages made her claustrophobic."

"Well, there you are, then."

"I don't think so. Something more than claustrophobia was happening. It was as if she was in the garage with someone else, someone who scared her. She didn't *see* me, G.I. At least not for a few minutes." He blew out a gusty sigh. "I don't know. Maybe I'm overreacting."

"Maybe. Maybe not. You gotta go with your gut."

"My gut says she was having some kind of flashback. When she snapped out of it, she was embarrassed. She didn't come inside."

"She ran?"

"Yeah."

"I hear your worry. You're thinking she'll keep on running and leave you and Zoey in the wake."

"Maybe I am, G.I. I don't know. I like her a lot." There. He'd admitted the truth—as if G. I. Jack hadn't guessed fifteen minutes ago. "I haven't felt anything this strong for a woman in a long time. I tried with Margo, but—"

"Your heart was never in that relationship, son. Everyone knew that but you. Even Margo."

"Probably. I feel bad about that. Margo's a good woman."

"Best thing you could have done for Margo

was to let her go. She and the city manager had dinner last night at the steak house. They looked mighty cozy."

"No kidding?" Now, that was good news. He didn't feel quite so guilty now.

"Margo wasn't the right woman for you and Zoey. Not from the git-go."

"Are you trying to say Cheyenne is?"

"Not saying anything of the kind, but she might be. Besides, that gal needs you, Doc. You can help her. I feel it right here." He tapped his sternum again, this time with the butt of the knife. The thought crossed Trace's mind that he was glad to have his vet supplies in the truck in case G.I. wounded himself.

"God put her in my path for a reason."

"Maybe more than one reason. Could be you need her, too."

Trace didn't need any reminders. His brain was giving him enough fits. Even when Cheyenne wasn't in the room, he thought he smelled her very subtle perfume. And last night, when she'd sat across his dinner table, making small talk and looking too pretty for words, he'd wanted her to stay there. She was getting under his skin in a powerful way.

"Where's Popbottle Jones this morning?"

G.I. gave him an amused look as if to say he wasn't fooled by the intentional topic shift. He plopped the slab of cheese into a baggie and slid

174

the zipper shut. "Here ya go. Enough there for Miss Cheyenne, too."

Trace lifted his eyes toward the ceiling, and the old man chuckled, the sprouts of hair at his ears jiggling.

G. I. Jack shuffled to the fridge, opening the door. Hand braced on the upper edge, he bent forward and rummaged around. "Popbottle went over to the—"

A stomping, clattering noise drowned out the rest of his answer. Ulysses Jones came through the back door. A plastic shopping sack crinkled as he set it on the table next to Zoey's cheese. The tops of two paint cans, one red and one black, poked out.

"Ah, our good veterinarian, I see. Biscuit informed me of a visitor." Popbottle chuckled. "Poor soul refused to come out from under the porch. I should have known you were the cause."

Trace shrugged. "Sorry about that."

"Not an issue, I assure you." Popbottle fished in the bag and came out with a can of coffee and three badly bruised bananas. "For all his fierce-some size, Biscuit is of a timid disposition. By the time his next appointment arrives, you will have returned to best friend status."

G.I. pointed a finger at Trace. " 'Specially if you give him one of them doggy vitamins. He's fond of the liver flavor."

"I'll keep that in mind." Trace pushed up from the table. "I need to get moving, boys, if Petunia's milk is ready."

Popbottle Jones dropped into a chair and swiped a hand across his brow. "What did you think of Cheyenne's heroics? A bit foolhardy, if you ask my opinion, which you did not, but I must say our girl is full of spunk."

"Yep." G.I. plunked a gallon jar of goat's milk on the already crowded table. "Spunky."

"I'm not surprised, though, were you? From the very first day we met, I told G.I. she was deep water, very deep water. Didn't I, G.I.?"

G. I. Jack's head bobbed. "You sure did. Deep water, he said. Real deep water."

Trace looked from the bobbing army cap to the heavy bags under the eyes of Popbottle Jones. "You've lost me, boys. I don't know what you're talking about. What happened?"

"I thought G.I. would have informed you by now." Popbottle cast a censorious look at the other man.

G. I. Jack shrugged. "Nope. Wasn't my story to tell."

"Tell me what?" Trace leaned one elbow on the countertop and reached for his half-empty coffee cup. Popbottle would tell the story in his own way in his own time frame. No amount of prompting would hurry him along. The exiled professor loved to practice his long-unused oratory skills.

"Last night at the Redemption Motel, your lovely and able employee accosted an angry drunk with overactive fists."

Trace choked on his coffee. G. I. Jack slapped him on the back, an action that did nothing but thrust him forward so the nanny goat could stick her nose in his coffee cup.

Sputtering, he asked, "Is she all right?"

Popbottle went on to tell the story of a runaway wife tracked down by a gorilla of an abusive, alcohol-soaked husband and how Cheyenne stepped in to defend the woman.

"I knew she had it in her," G. I. Jack said, head bobbing. "Yes, sir, I knew it. See, I told you, Doc. She's a good 'un."

"Where did you hear this?" And why hadn't anyone informed him?

"Our comely Widow Wainright was on the scene as well. She went to the sheriff first thing this morning to make an official report in case the man returns. Miriam Martinelli was delivering breakfast for the inmates and overhead."

"And now the incident is all over town?"

"Correct."

Trace figured the story had grown in proportion from the actual event, but his blood ran cold at the thought of Cheyenne facing down an enraged drunk. He'd seen her afraid and vulnerable and shaking like a sick kitten. How had she mustered the courage to do such a thing?

"You're positive she's all right? He didn't hurt her, did he?"

Earlier, when he had opened the clinic, Cheyenne had not yet arrived. Now his stomach twisted to think she might be at the motel, alone, scared, maybe injured. He remembered the way she'd trembled against him that night in the garage. Now there was no one at her apartment to protect and comfort her.

He wasn't a violent man, but if some jerk put his hands on Cheyenne there was going to be more trouble than anyone had ever seen out of Trace Bowman.

The memory of Ray Madden and a mangled Yorkie flashed through his head. "Who was this creep? And why was Cheyenne involved? Why didn't someone call the police? What was going on over there?"

Popbottle gave him a long, searching look. "Simmer down, son. From all reports, she survived the disturbing encounter unharmed."

"Put the rascal out on his ear." G. I. Jack smacked his lips together in satisfaction. "That's what I heard. Tossed him right out like a bag of garbage."

Coffee splashed out as Trace thunked his cup on the counter. The story worsened with every telling. "What was she thinking?"

Both men turned to look at him.

"Apparently not of herself," Popbottle said.

"She was concerned for the other woman. Courageous, if somewhat foolhardy."

Trace couldn't wrap his head around the story. Sure, Cheyenne was tough, but she was fragile, too. A drunk was especially dangerous. She could have been killed.

His gut twisted at the notion. He thrust an agitated hand to the back of his head.

He asked again, "Why weren't the police called?"

"That, my boy, is a very reasonable question."

"And one I intend to ask."

The next thing Trace knew he was out the door and in his truck.

Popbottle Jones stood in the doorway, patting Gravy's intrusive head as the animal doctor roared away. "G.I.?"

G. I. Jack, munching a piece of goat cheese, ambled up for a look. "Yep?"

"I stopped by the library today."

"Wondered what took you so long."

"The World Wide Web is a fount of information. Did you know you can put your name in and find out all kinds of things?"

"No!" G. I. Jack looked horrified. "You didn't find my name, did you?"

"Yours was not the name that had me interested. I am fully aware of your former indiscretions as you are fully aware of mine. No need to resurrect the long-buried and forgiven."

"True." G.I. lifted his cap and scratched. "Whose, then?"

"Cheyenne Rhodes."

"Find out anything interesting?"

"Our lovely young heroine has a painful past."

"No surprise."

"She killed a man, G.I. Self-defense. Justifiable homicide in the line of duty. She was a police officer."

G.I. chewed a bite of cheese, thinking. "Must have been a bad criminal."

"One of the worst, a serial rapist who tortured his victims."

The implication hung in the air unspoken.

"You gonna tell Doc?"

Popbottle sighed as though the weight of knowledge was a heavy load. "I shall have to give the matter serious thought."

"He's falling for her."

"Which only adds to my concerns."

G. I. Jack clapped him on the shoulder. "Trace is a good man. He can handle it."

"I hope you're right, my friend. I hope you're right."

Chapter Eleven

Have you lost your mind?"

Cheyenne spun around at the sound of Trace's outraged words. He stormed into the exam room where she was clipping the nails on a shitzu, slammed the door behind him and strode toward her. She took a step back.

"What's going on?" Her gaze went to the closed door. She and Trace were alone inside this room. She should be nervous. Instead, she was thrilled to see him, even if he was furious about something.

He stopped in front of her, jaw pulsing with tension. "Why didn't you tell me?"

"Tell you what?"

"You know what. You should have told me yourself."

Fear and guilt and shame swept over Cheyenne like an avalanche. He knew. Just as she was beginning to hope again, he'd discovered the ugly truth about Dwight Hector—and her.

"How did you find out?" The words squeezed out through a throat tight with emotion.

He kept coming, moving into her personal space and closer. Cheyenne started to back away, bumped up against a table and stopped. Her heart was pounding like the hooves of a dozen race-horses, but she wasn't afraid of Trace Bowman. Quite the contrary.

"Did you think you could keep something as serious as this a secret? Redemption is a small town."

Why did he have to discover the ugly truth about her now? Last night with him and Zoey was the first time in months she'd felt whole. And now he knew she was anything but whole.

"I didn't want you to know."

"Why?"

Why? How could he ask a question like that? A brutal attack and . . . what came after . . . was not exactly dinner conversation.

"I—I—" She squeezed her eyes shut, willing away the overwhelming disappointment. He knew, and the death knell was sounding on a . . . friendship that had only begun. "I'm sorry."

"Sorry isn't enough. You have to promise me."

Hand at her throat, Cheyenne whispered, "Promise you what?"

Trace spoke through clenched teeth. *"Promise me."*

She had no idea what kind of promise he was trying to extract. Promise not to be attacked in her own garage? Promise to tell him every hor-rific detail of a night she couldn't bear to remember and yet couldn't forget?

"I don't know what you mean."

One minute she was holding a shitzu like a shield and in the next, she was yanked into Trace's arms, the dog pressed between them.

She should have been insulted. Instead she was stunned and more than a little thrilled. For the first time in a long while, she wanted to be in a man's arms. No, not any man's. Trace's.

Her stomach didn't roll and her blood didn't run cold. She didn't think of Dwight Hector's rancid breath or overpowering rage. She didn't think of the humiliation and pain.

She thought of nothing and no one but Trace Bowman, of the strong corded muscles of his arms tenderly cradling her against him, of his warm breath soughing against her hair.

"Cheyenne," he said in a half growl, half plea as though she was precious. The notion disarmed her. "I was—"

"You were what?"

"Scared."

"Trace," she murmured, hearing her no-nonsense voice turned to a quivery whisper. "I don't understand—"

"Shh. Just let me hold you. Let me know you're okay."

Why would he want to touch her now that he knew? Paul hadn't wanted to. Her loving fiancé had never even kissed her again afterward.

Could Trace possibly be different?

A terrible yearning rose in her, like a tattered kite reaching for the blue sky. A yearning to love, to be normal again, to believe that a man could see the real woman inside, not the victim of a brutal crime.

She could no more reject the tenderness flowing from Trace Bowman than she could change what had happened that fateful night. This kind, gentle man filled the empty chasm of her heart with an indescribable hope.

She leaned into him, pulse thrumming, emotions trembling.

"Tell me you're okay," he murmured, voice throaty and rough with masculine tenderness.

She would never be okay. She didn't even know what okay meant anymore. Didn't he realize that?

But for one moment in time when Trace smoothed her hair from her face and stroked her cheek with enough genuine concern to bring tears to her eyes, Cheyenne needed to believe healing was possible.

She shivered, not with fear and loathing, but with hope and longing. If she were a normal woman—

But she wasn't. And Trace knew that now. He knew her darkest secret and pitied her.

Trembling a little, she pulled back, drawing with her the unique scent of him—warm male and antiseptic, dogs and fresh outdoors.

The air-conditioning kicked in and the waft of cold air from the ceiling vents raised goose bumps on her arms. She shivered, clutching the stunned shitzu for warmth.

Trace reached for her again. She shook her head.

"You don't want to do that." But she wished he would.

"That's where you're wrong, tough girl." Fists on his hip bones, his intense blue gaze bored into her with laser power, but he didn't touch her again. As much as that hurt, she understood. "You could have been killed."

"I wasn't." Though there had been many times she'd almost wished she had been. The aftermath had been a kind of death. The person she'd been before no longer existed.

"Why didn't you call the police?"

"No time." She swallowed, sick with the pictures whirling through her memory. "Can we talk about this some other time?"

He moved in again. His chest rose and fell in agitation. "Not until you promise me."

"Okay. I promise." *Whatever. Just stop making me think about it.*

"Never—do you hear me?" He jabbed a finger into the space between them. "Never take on an abusive drunk again by yourself. Call the police. Call me. Call that shitzu in your arms. But don't bust in like Eliot Ness all by yourself. Domestic violence is nothing to monkey around with."

Cheyenne blinked, uncomprehending. She could hear the words but they made no sense. "What?"

"You. Last night. The drunk."

She stared at him, stunned. Relief drained the heat from her cheeks. He was talking about last night, not last year. He didn't know.

An exam table poked against her back. She wilted against the hard metal, and closed her eyes. "Thank goodness."

She felt him move, felt the stir of air as he came close again. A strong hand touched her face. She loved that. She loved his tender touch and warm compassion.

"Are you all right? You look pale."

"Never better."

When she opened her eyes, he was staring down at her with an expression that stopped the breath in her lungs.

"Don't play tough with me."

The shitzu wiggled. Glad for the excuse to look anywhere but at Trace, Cheyenne dropped her gaze and loosened her tight grip. "I'm smashing this dog."

"I noticed." He took the animal and set him on the floor. The shitzu waddled away, casting troubled glances at the vet and his helper.

Cheyenne gripped the table with one hand. Her knees were abnormally wobbly today. "You heard about the incident at the motel."

Trace tilted his head, giving her a curious look. "Isn't that what we've been talking about for the past five minutes?"

No. She moistened lips gone as dry as the sand. "Who told you?"

"Popbottle Jones."

"Whatever he said must have scared you. The situation really wasn't that bad." Right. And she threw up in the bushes like that all the time.

"Promise me, Cheyenne."

"Does it really matter?"

"Oh, yes. It matters." He reached for her again, but seemed to think better of touching her again, and let his hands fall helplessly to the side. "I don't want you hurt."

The notion sent a disturbing stab of sorrow to a heart she'd thought too scarred to penetrate. She didn't want him hurt, either, but he would be if he knew. They both would be. Maybe Zoey, too.

The stab went deeper. Trace still did not know the worst about her. If he did, the past three glorious minutes in his arms would never have occurred.

Somehow, in the short space of time, with his innate kindness and Pollyanna attitude, Trace Bowman had found a crack in her armor.

She was falling in love with her boss.

The jubilant realization was quickly replaced by searing sorrow.

187

"They said you took on an abusive drunk single-handedly. Why did you do that?"

Cheyenne battled and conquered the tide of emotions washing through her. A cop either got tough or took the ugliness of humanity home with her at night. She'd done both.

"Emma was crying. Bleeding. I had to do something."

Trace's blue eyes registered horror. "So the jerk was Ray Madden, oversize dog stomper. And he'd been hitting his wife."

If Trace was horrified by hitting, how would he react to what had happened to her?

Not well, she was sure. He was a Christian, holy and pure. A violent personal crime would send him running for the nearest exit.

Disappointment rose in her throat with the nasty taste of bile. She swallowed it back. No use getting soft. Life was what it was. That was why she was here in Redemption instead of investigating crimes in Colorado Springs.

Putting on her best tough-girl facade, she jacked a rueful eyebrow. "Abusers generally hit their victims."

"That's so far out of my mind-set, I can't go there."

How well she knew. "A lot of women go there on a regular basis."

"Was Emma hurt badly?"

"Just roughed up from what I could tell." She

bit down on her bottom lip, caught herself and stopped. "The scene was ugly. I'm worried about what he may have done after they left."

"She went with him?"

"I thought Popbottle Jones told you."

He rubbed a hand over the back of his neck. "I didn't actually wait around to hear the entire story."

Some of the tough-girl starch seeped out of her, and that pesky glow of pleasure crept in again.

"According to Kitty, Emma comes to the motel with some frequency. If she comes again, and I know about it, I'm going to help her. Maybe next time I can convince her to leave the dirt-wad."

"For a tough girl, you've got a big heart."

With a sniff of contempt, she tossed her head. "I don't like bullies."

"But that doesn't mean you have to take them on single-handedly."

"There was no one else around."

"My point exactly. Your courage is admirable but you could have been hurt."

"Next time, I'll get her away from him." She hoped. "Is there a women's shelter in Redemption? Or a safe house?"

"Not to my knowledge."

A wheel spun inside Cheyenne's head. When a woman needed to escape from an abuser, she needed a place to hide. She also needed a compassionate shoulder to cry on. If anyone understood that, Cheyenne did. The police force had sent her to counseling, but no one could relate to the trauma she'd suffered.

A surge of purpose flooded through her veins. She understood. She could relate. She was a former cop with know-how. If making a difference meant taking a risk—well, she had nothing left to lose.

Later that afternoon, Trace replayed the scene with Cheyenne over and over, wavering between awe and confusion. Thinking of nothing but her, he'd charged into the clinic and grabbed Cheyenne as if he had a right.

The second he'd touched her, a shower of sparks had erupted behind his eyelids and he'd temporarily lost his mind. He'd wanted to go on standing in the exam room with her in his arms for the rest of the day.

For a few amazing seconds, she'd melted into him as if she belonged there.

Emotions flew around inside him like a roomful of agitated parakeets. Trace didn't know where to go from here. Cheyenne was his employee, a wounded soul he'd wanted to help, but now he wanted more than that. He wanted her. He wanted her to trust him enough to share what had hurt her so badly. He wanted her to teach his daughter piano and eat his bachelor's popcorn. He wanted to make her smile, and he wanted to hold her in his arms again.

Man, did he have a lot of praying to do! He needed Somebody bigger and wiser to guide him through the minefield that was Cheyenne Rhodes.

"Dr. Bowman?"

Trace jerked his head up. "Yes?"

Jilly gazed curiously at him. He never failed to be amazed by the number of freckles dotting her nose. "Are you going to remove those staples or admire them?"

His focus returned to the hamster flopped on his back on the table. The relaxed little rodent had suffered a close encounter with the family cat. A pair of glazed, beady eyes stared up at him, accusing. "Are you gonna fix me or not?"

"Sorry. I drifted."

"I noticed. You've drifted a lot today. Is anything wrong?"

Everything was wrong. He was falling for a mystery woman who took risks. A woman who would probably run the other direction if she had any idea of the effect she was having on him. A woman who had also captured his daughter's heart.

"Everything's fine."

The door cracked open and Jeri poked her head inside. "Margo called. Something about a Chamber meeting today at noon."

He let out a groan. "I completely forgot."

"That's what she figured. She said it was no biggie. She'll send you the minutes."

G. I. Jack was right. He and Margo had parted amicably for good reason. They were never a match. He never remembered the things that mattered to her and vice versa. He hadn't understood the implication of that before. Now he did. Without Margo, life went on normally. If Cheyenne walked away, he would not be as accepting. And the notion scared him spitless.

He quickly finished the staple removal and returned the hamster to his owner. The little fella looked relieved to escape the distracted vet.

As Trace stepped into the hall, he bumped into Cheyenne. Her hands were loaded with medication boxes.

He reached out in reflex and caught her arms. His pulse accelerated like a Ferrari. Man, oh, man, something was definitely going on here.

"Hey."

She righted herself and stepped back. He didn't loosen his grip. He didn't want to. Her arms were fit and firm, the skin feminine and soft. But neither her skin nor her looks alone compelled him. It was *her*, a woman of strength and character and decency. Why else would she have defended another woman against a larger assailant? Why else would she be kind to his child and Toby and the myriad animals and people coming through his clinic each day?

That pesky little voice inside his head reminded him that something was very wrong in Cheyenne's world, no matter how courageous and kind she might be. He ignored the warning completely when his eyes met—and held—hers. Something warm and hopeful flickered within Cheyenne's nearly black irises.

"You okay?"

Her glance slid away. "Great."

She was on the defensive, her tough-girl face sliding into place like an invisible shield.

"Are you mad at me?"

"For what?"

"This morning." He shrugged. "You know. I came on pretty strong."

Her face softened. "I didn't see it that way."

Did that mean she liked being in his arms as much as he liked having her there?

"Good, because Zoey's spring concert is tonight. Want to come over for an early dinner?"

Where had that come from?

She looked as startled by the invitation as he felt. "Do you want me to?"

More than anything he could think of. "I wouldn't ask if I didn't want you to."

He held his breath, hopeful, but uncertain. Cheyenne was as unpredictable as Oklahoma weather.

"Is your mom cooking again?"

"Just me and Zoey and you."

She seemed to struggle with indecision and Trace's hopes began to tumble. He took some of the boxes from her hands. "Zoey is counting on you being at the concert. She made me promise to remind you. I also had to cross my heart, hope to die and stick a thousand needles in my eye."

Using Zoey was a dirty trick. He hoped it worked.

Cheyenne laughed. "Painful."

"Tell me about it. I've learned never to break a promise."

Her shoulders relaxed. "I think I promised, too. So in the spirit of avoiding needles in the eye, I'll say yes."

A shout went off inside his chest. *Down, boy. Be calm. It's only a dinner and a kid's concert.*

"Great. We'll toss some steaks on the grill. How does that sound?"

"Perfect. I can whip up a salad, maybe even a dessert if you like simple."

"You don't have to cook."

"What if I want to?"

"Then I would be stupid to refuse. We can cook together. It'll be fun."

Together. The word resounded in his brain. He and Cheyenne side by side, in his house, like a couple.

He could handle that.

"If you don't get called out."

"No house calls allowed on Zoey's Spring Concert night." He hoped.

"But what if someone needs you?"

"Then I will need you more than ever." The choice of words sent a ripple through him. "To video the concert, I mean."

"Sounds like a plan. I can do that if necessary."

"After the concert, if it's not too late, we'll come back home. Watch the video. Listen to Zoey tell every detail over and over and over again."

"And eat more of your chili-cheese popcorn?"

"It could happen."

Her mouth curved. "Promise?"

He crossed his heart with an index finger. "Hope to die and stick a thousand needles in my eye."

"You are a brave, brave man."

No, he wasn't all that brave, but he needed to move forward. And he was fairly certain Cheyenne Rhodes had something to do with getting his life off high center.

"It's a date, then. You, me, Zoey and dozens of singing, stomping kids."

"I guess it is."

His gaze never wavered from Cheyenne's face as they stood like two teenagers grinning at each other, flirting with their eyes.

Outside in the kennels a dog yipped, and up front a deeper dog voice responded.

But they were not teenagers. He was a single

dad familiar with tragedy, and she was a woman of secret sorrows. If they had any hope of moving the relationship forward, Cheyenne had to open her heart and trust him.

A date. Trace had asked her on a real, bona fide date.

Okay, so the date was more for his daughter than for him, but the sense of anticipation brewing all afternoon was nothing short of breath-stealing.

After the moments in his arms that morning, she'd thought nothing could be better. She'd been wrong. The promise of normalcy, of spending personal time with a man that she liked and respected started a melody in her head that wouldn't stop. A melody that crowded out the ugly, persistent memories.

She'd eaten meals with Trace before. She'd been to his home any number of times. Tonight, however, was different. Tonight he was a man. She was a woman. This was a date.

With the scent of beef sizzling on the air, Cheyenne roamed around Trace's spacious backyard past an aboveground pool that was still covered for the winter. Two puppies and a big, shaggy mutt followed. She'd never had a pet, but Zoey's animals were sweethearts. Like the child herself. And the dad.

"When do you open the pool?"

"Usually the end of May. Why? Want to go swimming tonight?" He pumped his eyebrows. "We could always go down to the river and take a dip."

She laughed. "And freeze ourselves half to death. Besides, we have a concert to attend."

"I meant after the concert."

"In the dark?"

"Where's your sense of adventure?"

"Check back with me in July. I'm sure I'll be more adventurous in hundred-degree weather."

"I'll do that. Only, Zoey will have nagged me into uncovering our pool by then."

"Is she a good swimmer?"

"Excellent, but she's the reason our pool is aboveground."

"To reduce the chance of her falling in accidentally?"

"Right. She has to climb the ladder on purpose to get in the water. Drowning is not an option."

"You're such a good father." He couldn't have an easy time raising a daughter alone, especially one with special needs. But he kept up on all the latest advancements for blind children, even belonged to a support group, all while juggling his extremely busy animal practice, church activities and civic duties.

"I'm trying." His dimple-activating grin appeared. "Come on. The steaks are nearly done."

She followed him into the house where Zoey

was painstakingly setting the table. "Need any help?"

The child lifted her face, her left ear tilted toward Cheyenne. "I think I have everything. Don't I?"

"Yes. How did you know which bottle was steak sauce?"

"The shape." Zoey elevated her shoulders in a cute shrug. "When I'm not sure I open the lid and sniff."

"Smart girl."

Trace set a plate of steaks on the table. Cheyenne and Zoey had already prepared the salad and bread. "All we need is drinks."

"I'll get them, Daddy." Zoey opened a cabinet door, took down three glasses and filled them with water. Cheyenne resisted the urge to rush in with assistance. Taking her cues from Trace, she understood how Zoey had become so self-sufficient and confident. Trace allowed her to do things for herself. If she spilled or made a mistake, he didn't make a big deal of it.

Smiling, Trace drew a chair away from the table and nodded for Cheyenne to be seated. She tried, and failed, to remember the last time she'd allowed a man to hold her chair. He repeated the courtesy for his daughter, adding a flourish and a wisecrack that made her giggle.

Trace Bowman was a special man.

Throughout dinner, the atmosphere vibrated

with Zoey's excitement about the coming concert. The conversation ebbed and flowed with ease, from a discussion of the new large animal pens Trace was having built at the clinic to general talk about Redemption and the townspeople.

A couple of times, the past tried to crowd out her pleasure, but she fought the memories down. Just for tonight, she was determined to forget and to pretend that she was a normal woman having a normal date with an extraordinary man.

As soon as the meal ended, Zoey rushed to her room to get ready. Cheyenne began clearing away the dishes.

"You don't have to do that," Trace's warm baritone said, close to her ear.

Her head swiveled toward him. Her pulse stuttered. He was impossibly, wonderfully close. So near that she could count his eyelashes. Amazingly, she felt no threat, no compunction to escape. She felt . . . happy.

"I don't mind." She hitched her chin toward the table. "Grab those plates and I'll rinse them."

"Bossy." When she shot him a mock frown, he grabbed the stack of plates and thrust them at her. "But I like bossy women."

She made a harrumphing sound. "Zoey's right. You're silly."

"Is that a good silly or a bad silly?"

"Good silly, Daddy." Zoey traipsed into the

kitchen wearing a white blouse, a black skirt and Mary Jane shoes. "Cheyenne and me likes you a bunch. Don't we, Cheyenne?"

What else could she say? "I guess we do."

Trace lifted one eyebrow and laughed. "Trapped like a rat in a maze?"

She couldn't resist. "Or not."

She waited for him to catch her meaning, enjoying his look of pleased surprise.

"Zoey and me likes you a bunch, too. Don't we, Zoe?" he said, eyes dancing.

"Yep." Oblivious of the undercurrents she'd created, Zoey hopped onto a chair and held out a hairbrush. "Cheyenne, will you fix my hair?"

"Be glad to." Right after her insides stopped smiling. Trace's words tumbled around in her brain like numbers in a lottery bin. He liked her a bunch. Was that a good thing or a bad thing?

Probably bad, but she just didn't want to deal with anything negative right now.

She took the brush and began to stroke Zoey's black silk curtain of hair.

She was enjoying herself. This man, this child, gave her something she'd been missing for a long time. They gave her hope.

The spring concert rocked!

Trace was wedged into a chair, his shoulders brushing Cheyenne on one side and Tooney Carter on the other. Tooney was the town mechanic whose daughter was in Zoey's class. Brushing shoulders with him didn't do a thing for Trace. Brushing shoulders with Cheyenne, however, was nice. Really, really nice.

A man was a pitiful creature. The things he would do to innocently be close to his woman of choice.

Along with the rest of the audience, he lifted his hands in applause as the third-grade classes took a bow. Cheyenne leaned over and whispered, "I think Zoey's up next."

Sure enough, the second graders traipsed on as the third graders departed. Zoey, head held high with confidence, came arm in arm with another child and found her place on the risers. His chest swelled with pride. Zoey was going to make it in life. No matter what he had to do, his little girl would find her way.

Cheyenne slanted another glance toward him, and he saw his pride reflected in her eyes. "Look at her. She's gorgeous."

"Yeah," he said.

The music director, stationed below the stage, tapped a count of three and the squeaky recorder music began. On a scale of one to ten, the sound was a two, but like the other parents there, Trace thought the kids were awesome.

When the time came for Zoey's solo, Trace reached for Cheyenne's hand and squeezed, praying for his child to do well. He knew, in the large scheme of things, a recorder solo of "If You're Happy and You Know It" wasn't all that important, but tonight doing well was important to Zoey.

Cheyenne returned the anxious squeeze, her gaze glued to the brightly decorated stage.

Along with a cacophony of stomping and clapping, Zoey executed the notes with perfect clarity.

Under his breath, Trace murmured, "Yes!"

After the concert, Trace and Cheyenne wove through the jammed auditorium to collect Zoey, who waited in the wings with her teacher.

"Here comes your dad," Mrs. McAlvaney said to her charge as Trace and Cheyenne approached.

Face alive with excitement, Zoey said, "And Cheyenne, too?"

Mrs. McAlvaney raised her eyebrows in question.

"I'm here, Zoey," Cheyenne said.

Zoey broke away from the teacher and rushed forward, slamming into Trace's knees. "Was I great, Daddy?"

"Greater than great."

"Can I have a hug?"

What an odd question. "Sure."

He went down to her level and gathered her to his chest.

She struggled back. "No, Daddy, a group hug.

202

You and me and Cheyenne, the way a family is supposed to be."

You and me and Cheyenne. A family.

With a twist in his heart, Trace knew his fear had come to pass. Zoey needed a mother, and she'd chosen Cheyenne.

Chapter Twelve

Ulysses Jones ambled up the curved drive from the main road toward the grand old Victorian the Hawkins family had owned since the Land Run. The rambling house sat on the other side of town from his place, much closer to the river, but walking was no problem for Ulysses. The Lord Almighty had granted him strong legs even into old age and he didn't mind using them.

For once, he didn't carry a knapsack full of recyclables. He carried a bouquet of lily of the valley.

The enormous maples cast a thick shade over Lydia Hawkins's yard and left his approach in shadow. She sat so still, there on the wicker porch bench, that he wondered if she was asleep. She looked in perfect peace and right where she belonged. Lydia had never lived anywhere but here.

To his eyes, she was still as pretty as sunshine. In a yellow dress and straw hat, she looked the way she had the first time he'd seen her.

He removed his ball cap, shoved the wad of cloth into the pocket of his jacket and ran a hand over his hair. He'd painstakingly oiled, combed and slicked back the unruly sprouts she'd once admired. Once, a long time ago, when they were both young, before he'd taken the wrong direction.

He sniffed at his underarm and grunted with satisfaction. Before leaving the house, he'd dabbed on men's cologne—an ancient bottle of phoo-phoo water, as G. I. Jack called it—and the scent still lingered above any perspiration created by the long walk.

"Is that you, Ulysses?"

He swallowed. She'd never called him Pop-bottle the way everyone else did. The nickname had begun during the cruel years of junior high when his neck had outgrown the rest of him. He no longer minded. In fact, he even embraced the pseudonym, but Lydia had never used it.

"Indeed, it is. Have you a spare moment for an old friend to come calling?"

"Always." And she told no lie. Lydia made time for everyone. One of her gifts was the powerful ability to make every single person feel as if he or she were the focus of her interest and her attention.

She pointed toward a pretty wicker chair. "Have a seat."

He did so, gripping the bouquet against his belly.

"The flowers are beautiful. Lily of the valley."

He held them out toward her. "Are they still your favorite?"

Lydia nodded. "Your mind always amazes me. How you remember such trivia, I'll never know."

Though his intellect was significant, he would never consider anything about Lydia Hawkins as trivial.

He noticed then the fatigue around her eyes and the slight breathlessness with which she spoke.

"The rumors are true, then," he said simply.

Lydia lifted the bouquet to her nose. "What rumors would that be?"

"About your health."

"I'm aging, Ulysses, in case you hadn't noticed."

He hadn't. "You're still a beautiful woman, but I can see you aren't well."

"Annie has been talking again?"

"Annie cares about you, but yes, we encountered one another at the post office yesterday. I asked. She told me."

"She's the finest nurse an old woman could have, but do you know she works day and night to care for those children of hers?"

"If Joey Markham had been a man, she wouldn't have to." Annie had married on the rebound. The results had been disastrous. Now she was alone with two children to support.

"If only she and Sloan—" Lydia bit her lip and paused.

Ulysses knew he was treading on sensitive ground, but he asked anyway. "Tell me about Sloan. Does he know how sick you are? Have you been in contact?"

Golden-brown eyes stared off down the drive as if Sloan would come racing home at any moment. "He knows."

Ulysses could see from the set of her jaw that she was not going to discuss Sloan. Not even with him. The ostracized nephew she'd loved like a son had not been back to Redemption in years. Most likely he would never return, not even when Lydia died.

The notion scraped his soul like barbed wire. He and Lydia were both aging. Time stood still for no man or woman, but God was faithful and just. When the body was no longer useful, the sweet Almighty stepped in.

But not Lydia, Lord. Not Lydia.

Since his return to Redemption years ago, Ulysses had made this trek at least once a month.

Though neither ever mentioned what had happened between them all those years ago, Lydia had long ago forgiven him. Sloan may have forsaken her, but Ulysses never would again.

"Tell me the news, Ulysses."

True to Lydia's nature, she never dwelled on sorrow or past mistakes. If she was dying, she would die with joy and grace.

So he told her the news. Of the construction of the new gymnasium, of the bass tournament for kids, of friends and neighbors, births and sicknesses. When he told her about Cheyenne Rhodes, she frowned slightly and promised to pray. He had no doubt she would. And God would hear.

After a bit he saw her wearing down. She pretended differently, but he knew.

"Would you like to hear a poem?" he asked, sliding a thin brown volume from his jacket.

She nodded. "No one reads poetry the way you do, in that rich, elegant voice. I've always loved your voice, you know."

He knew, but pride swelled inside his chest. Pride and concern. The short speech had cost her dearly. Though she'd sidestepped his queries about her health, he heard the raspy breathlessness and saw the pallor of her skin.

He flipped open the well-worn book. "Wordsworth?"

With a nod, she smiled and leaned her head

back against the bench, lily of the valley clutched in her hands like the bride she'd never been.

Professor Ulysses E. Jones lifted his best orator's voice and entertained the woman who had held his heart for more than fifty years.

The battered woman arrived at Cheyenne's apartment Saturday afternoon, announcing her presence with a timid rap.

Cheyenne tossed a bright red T-shirt into a pile of dirty laundry and went to the door, grabbing the Glock on her way. Sure, she was paranoid. Probably always would be.

This morning, at Trace's request, she'd taken Zoey shopping for summer clothes. She'd had a blast. Since the spring concert when Zoey had made the remark about family, Cheyenne had tried to back away, but she couldn't. The promised piano lessons had begun and even if they hadn't, she liked being with the effervescent child almost as much as she liked being with Zoey's dad.

She was getting in deep with her boss and his daughter. Self-preservation said run while she could because being with Trace made her too happy.

She stank at self-preservation.

An ear to the door, she said, "Who is it?"

A near whisper answered, "Emma Madden. You helped me the other night—"

Cheyenne yanked at the knob, immediately alert to the danger. Standing to one side, on guard, she ushered the slender woman inside while scanning the area beyond before she shut and locked the door.

She spun, taking in the white complexion and heavy makeup. "You're hurt."

Tears filled Emma's eyes. She ducked her head, ashamed. Brown hair fell over a dark bruise along her cheekbone. She wore long sleeves, a sure sign to Cheyenne that more bruises of varying colors resided beneath.

"I'm okay. I just had to get away for a little while and talk to someone." Her voice was barely above a whisper, as though she feared her husband would hear. "He says he's sorry but he keeps on doing it."

Cheyenne placed a careful hand on Emma's arm. The small woman trembled. "He'll go on hurting you, Emma. You need to get away from him, at least until he gets some help."

Shoulders slumped, Emma stared at the floor. "I can't."

"Can't or won't?"

"If I try to leave, he'll find me. Then there's no telling what he might do."

Cheyenne sat down on the end of the bed and motioned for Emma to take the chair.

Precautions first.

"Does he know where you are right now?"

"Oh, no. He'd get really mad if he knew I'd come back here." Her fingers tightened on the wooden chair arm. "I promised him I wouldn't."

Cheyenne relaxed the slightest bit. At least, the bozo wouldn't come charging in with drunken fists flying. "He *made* you promise?"

A hesitation before a whispered "Yeah."

The knowledge that the promise was extracted with a pound of flesh started a slow burn in Cheyenne's gut. She despised bullies. "What did you tell him?"

"Ray has poker on Saturday afternoon. I left a note saying I went to the library in case he comes back early. He never does, but—"

She didn't have to finish. Cheyenne knew the rest. If he returned to find her gone without a word, she'd pay dearly.

"I like to read. Sometimes Ray gets mad and rips up my books, but sometimes he doesn't care if I go the library."

"As in after he gets drunk and beats you up? Then he's sorry and tries to make up by buying you things or letting you see friends or go places. Right?"

Emma's head came up. The ghastly bruise on her cheekbone was more visible beneath the overhead light. "How did you know?"

"Unfortunately, you aren't the first case of domestic violence I've encountered. And I doubt if you'll be the last. Mean-fisted losers are everywhere."

"Ray says he loves me, but I don't know anymore. Lately, everything I do makes him mad. He says if I'd just learn my lesson he wouldn't lose his temper."

"No one has a right to hit you. Not even your husband. *Especially* your husband."

"I've been thinking a lot about that. About what you said that night and how you stood up to Ray. No one stands up to Ray, especially when he's drinking."

"Are you ready to leave him?"

"I can't. I have no money. No place to go."

"Ray controls the bank accounts?"

"Everything is in his name. He says I'm not smart enough to keep up with finances."

"Do you have kids?" Having a child complicated matters. She'd have a much harder time escaping and an even harder time keeping Ray away from her.

"Not yet." Emma gnawed her lip, her hands twisting in her lap. "You saw what he did to my dog. If he got mad, he might hit the baby. I don't want to get pregnant until we get things worked out."

Cheyenne didn't hold out much hope for that to happen. A man like Ray had to *want* to change. "Smart thinking." Probably the smartest thing the woman had done in a long time.

"I kept hoping things would get better. Ray can be sweet for days and I think everything is finally going to be okay."

"And then something sets him off."

Emma nodded, eyes bright with unshed tears. "It's my fault. I know when he's getting mad, but I can't seem to keep my mouth shut and do what he says anymore."

"Ray has issues that have nothing to do with you, Emma. He would have them no matter what you did or didn't do. How long have you been married?"

"We've been together since I was sixteen. He was twenty." She gave a self-conscious laugh. "I was flattered that an older guy liked me. And then we started dating and . . ." Her voice fell away. "You know. Fell in love, I guess."

"Has he always been like this?"

"Yeah. Pretty much."

"When did he start hitting you?"

"He gets real jealous. At first, I felt special because he loved me so much. But if a guy at school looked at me or talked to me, he'd get mad. We'd fight and—you know. After a while, I quit school. I thought things would get better."

"They didn't."

"No. Worse." Her hands twisted until they were red. "Ever since then . . . He always says he loves me so much, he goes a little crazy."

Cheyenne bought the crazy part. The love was another matter. "Do you believe that?"

"Not anymore. But I'm scared. He'll kill me if I leave."

"Will you talk to the police? I'd go with you."

Emma stiffened. "No. No. I didn't come here for that. Ray would find out and—" She started to rise. "After the other night, I thought—I don't know what I thought. I'm just stupid. Too stupid for anything. Maybe I should go."

Cheyenne sighed. The story was a common one. Women were too scared to leave, too distrustful of the legal system and helpless otherwise. What Redemption needed was a shelter, a place where women could hide, heal and start over again.

"Don't go, Emma. I won't push you to do anything you aren't comfortable with, but you should know something."

Emma teetered, one hand on the chair arm though her body tilted toward the door. "What?"

"I'm a former police officer."

Her mouth formed a round circle. "That's why you have a gun. And you weren't afraid to stand up to Ray."

"Yes."

"Wow." She breathed the word. "Have you ever shot anyone?"

A pause while Cheyenne considered the wisdom of answering that question. "A police

213

officer never wants to use deadly force."

"But you have."

Cheyenne sidestepped. "I've worked domestic violence cases for years. Trust me, I've seen some ugly stuff. You need to get away before he puts you in the hospital or worse."

"No one hires a tenth-grade dropout."

Cheyenne saw her point, and Ray probably fed into her low self-esteem by reminding her that she was uneducated.

"Don't you have family who can assist?"

Emma shook her head. "My mom says I made my bed and now I have to sleep in it. I think she's scared of Ray, too." Her gaze slid nervously around the room. She stood, dusting her palms down the sides of pink capris. "I don't know why I came."

When she moved toward the door Cheyenne caught her arm. Emma flinched and the reaction infuriated Cheyenne so much she was determined not to let Emma be hurt again. "I do. You came because you know being abused is wrong. You know you're in danger and you want help. Why don't you stay here with me until we figure out the next step?"

"Ray would find me and go crazy. He might hurt us both."

A quiver of fear pushed up inside Cheyenne's head, but she refused to consider the danger. Inside, she was still a police officer and she still had the Glock she'd promised never to use again.

She might have to break that promise. "If I find a place for you to stay, will you go there?"

"I don't know. I'm not sure what to do."

"You could start with a restraining order."

"I know how those work. I've watched TV. Men walk right past them and kill their wives."

Sadly, Emma was correct. A woman was most at risk of being murdered when she left her abuser. The harder she tried to keep him at bay, the angrier he would become. At least at first. Cheyenne had worked several such cases and was sickened by the memory of murders and murder-suicides. "You said Ray takes care of the money. But do you have access to the bank account or any money at all?"

"Yeah. For groceries and stuff."

"Can you start saving anything back? Even a little here and there?"

"I can try."

"If you can't, we'll deal with it. There are resources available. We just have to find them. I'm new to Redemption, but I know people who might help."

"You won't tell them my name, will you?"

"No, but I will muster every available resource. I already have ideas, but I need time to talk to people. Can you come back?"

Emma gnawed her lip. "I never know for sure. Well, except on Saturday when he plays poker."

"That's perfect. But don't come here. He knows about this place now. I'll meet you somewhere."

"The library?"

"Brilliant idea."

The small bit of praise brought a gleam of determination to Emma's face.

"I won't lie to you, Emma. Breaking away won't be easy. But if you're willing to try, I'll help you every step of the way."

"Why are you doing this? You don't even know me."

"Let's just say I've been in your shoes, in a manner of speaking. I know how it feels to be controlled and abused."

Those few hours had been unspeakably horrific. How did women survive years of abuse?

"Meet me at the library next Saturday afternoon. I'll get there early and reserve a study room. In the meantime, I'll explore your options. Safe houses, shelters, job training, whatever we can find around Redemption."

"You'd do all that for me?"

"People help each other here. At least, that's what someone told me when I first moved to Redemption." And she was starting to believe it.

If she could meet with Emma often enough, she would find a way to help her escape the abusive relationship. If nothing else, she could listen and advise. Her intervention training would come in handy.

"Will you come?"

Emma nodded. "If I can."

With a mild sense of accomplishment, Cheyenne said, "Good. That's a start. In the meantime, if anything happens, call me." She scribbled her phone number on a piece of paper. "There's a domestic violence hotline in the phone directory. They offer help, too."

Emma clutched the paper in her fingers as a drowning person clutches a lifeline. "I'm scared. What if Ray finds out?"

If the volatile Ray discovered her plan, she'd be a statistic, but Cheyenne didn't say that. "Emma, you've been playacting that everything is fine for a long time. You can pretend a little longer."

Determination straightened Emma's bent posture. "I'll try. I have to."

The frightened woman opened the door and started out. Halfway to her car she stopped and turned. "Cheyenne?"

"Yes?"

"I saw the sign on the motel." At Cheyenne's questioning frown, she clarified. "The Bible study. Will you ask them to—you know, pray for me?"

Pray. The single word dropped into Cheyenne's stomach with the weight of a bowling ball.

"Sure." What else could she say?

Chapter Thirteen

❧

Trace stood on the bank of Redemption River listening to Cheyenne worry out loud about the battered Emma Madden. Her instincts at that first meeting in the clinic had been correct. Ray Madden not only abused his dog; he beat his wife.

Now Emma had come to Cheyenne for help. The fact that Cheyenne had already endured a face-to-face encounter with the man didn't sit too well with Trace. But what could he do? Emma was desperate, and Cheyenne was not a woman to turn her back.

"How's she doing?"

"Apparently Ray has been in a good mood. Now she thinks they can work things out."

"In other words, he hasn't beaten her this week?"

"Right," she said grimly.

Trace clenched his teeth in suppressed fury. If there was one thing he despised, it was a man who used his superior size and strength to harm instead of protect. Now that his suspicions about Ray Madden had been confirmed he wanted to find the jerk and have a little man-to-man visit. "Do you think she'll return?"

"She said she would. I found a great book on domestic abuse that I want her to read, but I'm worried her husband will find out."

"I hope you'll exercise caution. If this guy discovers what's going on, he could cause big trouble."

"I know, but Emma's alone and scared. I'm going to do everything within my power to help."

The pure grit in her tone gave him pause. Cheyenne was the kind of woman who would throw herself in front of a speeding car to save someone. She might not know that about herself, but he did.

"You promised you'd be careful. I don't want you hurt." His voice sounded gruff.

"I can take care of myself."

"Oh, yeah, I forgot. Tough girl on duty." He hooked an arm around her neck and tugged playfully. "No two-hundred-fifty-pound man would dare stand up to you."

She twisted her head around, bringing her face tantalizingly close to his. His belly jitter-bugged in response.

She might have her mind on Emma, but he had *his* mind on her. He'd been yearning to kiss her for a while, though common sense had said to take things slow. The last thing he wanted to do was scare her away.

But that didn't stop him from thinking.

Now, here they were, just the two of them on the river bridge watching the sunset over the water. Fingers of orange and purple shot up into the sky like fireworks and promised a spectacular show. With Zoey attending a birthday party at the Pizza Palace, the time alone was a rare gift.

He bumped his forehead against Cheyenne's.

"Under that tough-girl facade," he teased, "beats the heart of a cupcake."

"Well, this cupcake wishes she could do more than sit at the library and talk. Emma's jerk of a husband is a ticking time bomb. I want her out of there."

"Gotta be her choice."

Cheyenne moaned. "I know."

His admiration ratcheted higher with each new layer of Cheyenne he encountered. Her dark beauty had attracted him, but the woman beneath the armor brought a song back into his heart that had gone silent the day he'd buried Pamela.

He'd tried to find the melody in his work, his friends, even his relationship with the Lord, but not until Tough Girl strode into his clinic and shoved puppies in his face did he fully understand what had been missing.

"You know what?"

She tilted her face toward him. "What?"

He moved closer, glad when she didn't back away, and looped his arms lightly around her, letting his clasped hands ride easily at her lower back. He waited, holding his breath, expecting the defensive wall to shoot up between them. When he met no resistance, his heart banged against his rib cage with such force he was sure she could feel the thunder. "I think you're an amazing woman."

She swallowed. The hard edge of wariness softened. The change was slight, but Trace was so in tune with Cheyenne's expressions, he recognized the difference.

He canted toward her, hoping, wondering, and yet careful.

"You're pretty amazing yourself," she murmured.

That was all the encouragement Trace needed. With a smile rising up in his chest, he kissed her.

The shock of Trace's warm mouth touching hers went through Cheyenne in waves. She expected to be repulsed. Instead, she melted against him like chocolate in the sunshine. Her hands moved up to caress the back of his neck and draw him closer. She'd been in Trace's arms before, but this was different.

She gave herself up to the emotion, putting her all into the kiss. Trace made a soft sound in the back of his throat and loosened his hold, bringing his hands up to cup her face.

Never had Cheyenne been kissed with such

beauty. His touch spoke of tenderness mixed with yearning and just enough passion to remind her that, beneath the rape victim, she was still very much a woman.

The seed of joy withered.

Rape victim. The words reverberated inside her skull, bouncing off the bones. Ugly images intruded.

Those few seconds in Trace's arms had drowned out the ugliness. But now the truth of who she was returned, a cruel reminder that Trace Bowman deserved more than she could ever be.

She allowed herself the luxury of a few more lovely seconds in Trace's arms. Time to capture the moment, to memorize the texture of his skin, the way his eyelashes lay against his cheekbone, the way he made her feel whole again. She'd need this memory.

Slowly, reluctantly, Cheyenne pulled away. Emptiness rushed in like a chill. She crossed her arms over the ache and turned to face the muddy river.

Her heart banged against her throat with enough force to make her cry. She wouldn't, though. No more tears.

She pressed a hand to her larynx to hold back the threatening sobs.

The soft crush of damp grass brought Trace to her side. She didn't look at him.

"Did I do something wrong?" His voice was quiet, serious, concerned. And, yes, a little hurt.

The tears tried again, pushing hard.

She hated this. Trace deserved better than a broken woman's rejection. "No. Nothing. Don't think that. You could never—"

With one finger, he touched her cheek. She closed her eyes against the tenderness.

"What, then?" he murmured.

"The problem isn't you. It's me."

He traced the curve of her cheek, the line of her jaw. She could feel his eyes boring into her, trying to understand what she could mean. "I care about you, Cheyenne."

That's exactly what she was afraid of. He wouldn't care if he knew.

Tell him, a voice screamed. Tell him and watch the light die in those gorgeous blue eyes. Watch the quick withdrawal as he searches for a way out of a relationship he never should have begun. Tell him and get the agony over with.

She opened her mouth, and to her horror the tears won, gathering at the corners of her eyes to mock her.

She angled her body away so he couldn't see. His hand fell away from her cheek, but she could feel him there, watching her, hurting a little, bewildered.

Crouching, she plucked a tiny purple wild-flower and pressed the delicate bloom to her nose. Her hands trembled, betraying her.

Trace stood behind, but she could feel his probing gaze like a heat at her back.

Out on the muddy red river, a broken tree branch headed downstream, caught in the strong current of spring rains. She remembered the story of converts who claimed the river washed their sins out to sea.

God, if it were only true, I'd jump in right now.

"Chey?"

The shortened version of her name spoke of familiarity and connection. He thought he knew her. Poor man.

"I know something's wrong. I've known since the moment you walked into my clinic with a box of puppies and a bad attitude. You can trust me."

She wanted to. Oh, how she wanted to. "I wish I could believe that."

"You can."

He hadn't a clue.

She might as well tell him. Tell him and end their . . . friendship right here and now.

She tossed the flower away. The tiny blossom fell into the mud, ruined. The muck of life had a way of ruining people, too. She didn't want her muck to soil Trace and Zoey.

Dusting her fingertips, she stood, though she couldn't look at Trace. "I was a police officer

224

before I moved here. A detective in special investigations."

Trace remained quiet. She could feel him listening, trying to make sense of the revelation. "I don't want you to hate me."

"Won't ever happen." When she didn't continue, he probed. "Tell me what you're afraid of, Cheyenne. I know something has hurt you and trust doesn't come easy. I know you sleep with the lights on."

"Kitty is a tattletale."

No, that wasn't true. Kitty had become a good friend, a woman to trust, a woman who prayed for her every day. Kitty had told Trace out of concern.

"And I saw you fall apart that night in my garage."

Her jaw tightened. He *would* have to bring that up.

"I also know you are an incredibly caring woman. Whatever happened was not your fault."

"You have no idea what you're saying, Trace. None."

"Then tell me. Trust me. I'm not going anywhere."

Oh, yes, he would. "I want to. I hate what this has done to me."

"Whatever happened can't be that terrible, can it?"

She watched the broken branch, now thirty yards downstream, for another second, then sucked in a breath of muddy river air and turned to meet his concerned gaze. "I killed a man."

Shock hit Trace like a Taser. Electrical impulses shot through his arms, down his spine and tingled his legs.

So this was the issue that had driven Cheyenne from her home and family.

As though equally stunned by her admission, the sun dropped below the horizon. The hazy gray of twilight surrounded them. They'd missed the last few glorious moments of sunset, but romance had faded from Trace's mind.

Help me, Lord. Give me the right words to say. Don't let me fail.

Cheyenne was already beating herself to a pulp over this. If he overreacted or said the wrong thing, she might retreat behind the wall and never come out again.

"Want to explain that a little further?"

She shrugged, trying to be nonchalant. Her tough-girl pose was back in place. He recognized the posture. She was hurting, throwing up the defense to keep from feeling.

"He was a slimeball." Her nostrils flared. Trace spotted the flame of anger, leashed but lurking. "I shot him in the line of duty."

"Then why are you tormented? Don't cops know they may be called upon to use deadly force?"

"Yes."

"Then why?"

"The D.A. filed charges against me for the use of excessive force."

"Was it? Excessive, I mean?"

"The jury didn't think so."

"There you are, then."

"You don't understand, Trace. I killed a man. And I didn't call 9-1-1 until he drew his last breath. Until I was certain he was dead."

Even in the growing darkness, Trace saw the moisture in her eyes. He also saw the anger. Part of him wanted to ask about the criminal. What did the man do? Why had she shot him and then hesitated to call 9-1-1? Though, he was certain there was more to this story, some instinct held him back from asking.

"Hey." He could no more keep his hands off her than he could drain this river with a teacup. "Come here."

Shaking her head, she crossed her arms. He was having none of it. She needed to be held. And he needed to hold her.

"I don't know what happened or why, but I'm not going away. And neither is God. He's not mad at you, Chey. He's here for you. And so am I. You don't have to be afraid anymore."

As if she'd longed to hear those exact words, her arms fell to her sides, all defenses crumbling. She looked wounded and bewildered and as fragile as dandelion puff.

"Come on, tough girl."

And as if totally defeated, she walked into his arms and laid her head against his chest.

Cheyenne rested her ear against the wild thud of Trace's heart. For all his outward calm, his inner motor raced and gave him away. The truth had shocked him.

Well, half the truth. She'd meant to tell the whole story, purge her soul and set him free, but in the end she'd lost her nerve. Trace's compassion was a formidable opponent. How did a woman fight against a man who refused to see her faults?

Night encroached. The willow trees cast dark, finger shadows across the water. Frogs, brave now in the protective dusk, set up their rhythmic croak. Her branch was gone, swept away to sea, though her sins remained here on the shore with a man who couldn't begin to comprehend true darkness of the soul.

Trace stroked her hair, letting his hand ride lightly at her neckline.

"Guilt is a mean companion," she murmured, letting him believe that remorse was the only emotion gnawing raw places inside her.

"A companion that causes night terrors and claustrophobia?"

She wasn't claustrophobic. And the fear of darkness had nothing to do with the plague of guilt, though responsibility for the event was an issue she had yet to resolve. Her world was no longer safe, either on the inside or the outside. Dwight Hector, dead or alive, had seen to that.

"When Pamela died," Trace said softly, "I felt guilty, although I couldn't have done anything to save her. Still, guilt and depression had a field day."

His situation was about as far from hers as a person could get, but he'd suffered grief and loss. He understood that much. "What did you do?" she asked.

He huffed. "Felt sorry for myself like a big baby."

In spite of the rampaging emotions and the tremble in her bones, a small laugh escaped. "No, you didn't."

"Did, too. But my parents are strong prayer warriors. Between them and a great big God who loves me more than I love Zoey—which is a lot—I came around."

Hope pinched up inside her. "How?"

"Mom poured scriptures into me. Even when I wanted her to go away, she'd sit next to me and read certain verses from the Bible, or she'd bring over a CD or a book on God's way of handling grief and loss. Pretty soon the Word soaked into my thick skull."

She shook her head and the movement made soft swishy sounds against Trace's cotton shirt.

"I don't know much about the Bible. I always thought of myself as a Christian, but somewhere along the line I sort of lost my way."

"All you have to know is that God loves you. He wants you healed and happy, and He's there for you, all the time."

Too simple. No one did something for nothing. Not even God.

"I haven't been all that holy, Trace. The night—" She stopped, started again. "That night, I'd had a few drinks before the shooting."

"And you wonder if the alcohol impaired your judgment."

"It happens."

"But that doesn't change God or the way He loves you. His forgiveness and peace and healing are still yours to claim. He wants to fix this, Cheyenne, if you'll let Him."

Like Emma, the ball was in her corner.

She'd tried everything else.

A car passed on the bridge, sending a brief sweep of yellow light across Trace's face.

Cheyenne's stomach quivered. Integrity, honor, decency flowed from Trace Bowman. She understood his earnest desire to see her healed. She felt the same way about Emma. Trace stirred a long-dormant seed of hope within her.

She touched his cheek, grasping at straws, afraid to believe and too lost not to try.

Long after she'd come back to the apartment, Cheyenne sat curled in the rose-colored armchair meditating on the evening's events. What had begun as a house call to deliver a colt had become a curious blend of romantic interlude and soul purging. Only she was not cleansed. The truth remained hidden, muddied now by half-truths and omissions. She was a trained cop. Taking out a criminal was an unpleasant, troubling, always regrettable part of the job, but cops do what they have to do. Contrary to what Trace now believed, the shooting wasn't what haunted her.

Ah, Trace. She sighed and leaned her head against the padded chair as her mind replayed the riverside scene.

She was not naïve. Trace had not needed her assistance to deliver the shiny, wobble-legged foal. He'd wanted to be with her. She could see his feelings growing, but the trouble was, those feelings were not for her. They were for the person he thought she was.

Instead of resolving the issue, she'd made the problem worse. Some deeply deluded section of her brain clung to hope with stunning tenacity.

Why couldn't she stick to her plan? If God had drawn her here, as everyone claimed, what was He trying to do? Give her a nervous break-down?

From the small table at her side, she took Kitty's dog-eared, underlined devotional. Her friend and landlady had given her the book the day Emma asked for prayer. With no real choice in the matter, Cheyenne had gone to Kitty's house to relay the message. What transpired afterward was still a mystery to Cheyenne.

Over fragrant cups of rose tea, time seemed to drift away, and before either realized, four of Kitty's faithful had gathered for more tea, crunchy sugar cookies and a lively discussion of the Bible. Though out of her element, Cheyenne had listened, saying little, but when the party broke up, Kitty thrust the book into her hands with orders to read something every night before going to bed.

So far, she'd ignored the advice.

The pocket-size book fit easily in her hands. She thumbed through, noted Kitty's tidy hand-printed comments on practically every page. This was a book Kitty loved. Why would she give it away?

As she turned another page, her attention fell to the words jotted along the margin. *I don't have to go through this alone. God is my refuge.*

Cheyenne could practically feel the anguish Kitty must have endured when her husband died. Yet here in this little book, she'd found solace.

Was solace, hope, healing really possible?

The prospect intrigued her so much she read the scripture printed on the page.

Come to me, all you that are weary and are carrying heavy burdens, and I will give you rest. Take my yoke upon you, and learn from me; for I am gentle and humble in heart, and you will find rest for your souls. For my yoke is easy, and my burden is light.

She'd heard that somewhere before, but where? She squinted in thought and the image of Redemption's Town Square materialized. Trace had taken her to the well, clearly expecting her to understand something she didn't.

Curious now with a strange lift beneath her rib cage, she reread the scripture. She certainly qualified as one of the weary. Dear God, she was tired of carrying around the heavy load of despair and shame. Even more tired of feeling sorry for herself. At some point, she had to get over this and move on.

. . . *and I will give you rest.*

She read that part four times. The promise was too easy. Surely God expected her to do something first, like build a church or give thousands that she didn't have to send missionaries to Africa.

She flipped to the next page and went on

reading, devouring the words as though they were medicine for a sickness. Maybe they were medicine. Medicine for a sick and floundering soul.

In His unfailing love, my God will come and help me.

Could God possibly love her after what had happened? She'd felt unclean and unworthy for a very long time.

She read the startling words again.

In His unfailing love, my God will come and help me.

Cheyenne's eyelids slid closed.

Oh, God, please come and help me.

But she'd prayed, even screamed those words a year ago in her own garage, and no one had come to help.

She shoved the thoughts aside, desperate to move away from that black night.

Come and help me, God. Give me rest. Let me sleep in peace. Make me feel safe again.

She wasn't sure how long she prayed and read and then prayed some more, but after a while she could no longer hold her eyes open to decipher the letters.

Whispering one final prayer, she climbed beneath the bedcovers and snapped off the lamp, sending the room into utter darkness.

Chapter Fourteen

～

Y ou've got that look."

G. I. Jack thumped a thick white mug on the table, talking loud enough that the mayor, the banker and three of Trace's patients turned from their hearty Sugar Shack breakfasts to gaze curiously at the vet.

Trace, himself nursing a cup of strong, black coffee and the beginnings of a headache, squinted at the old codger. "You mean the look that says I treated three coon hounds for copperhead bites before sunrise?"

His head felt like a hot air balloon, and he wondered if bug-eyed-from-exhaustion was the look G. I. Jack referred to.

"Ha. Not even close. You look that way every day."

Miriam appeared, topped off their coffee with a smile and moved on, alternately grousing at and teasing customers as she worked. That was Miriam, a mix of gruff and cranky, sweet and kind.

The Shack was packed as usual on a weekday morning. Smells guaranteed to cause Pavlov-type behaviors floated around the cramped bakery and friendly chatter competed with the clatter of cups and plates. A couple of fellas sat at the counter, perusing the morning paper, probably talking politics and baseball. Last he'd heard the Redemption Rogues had only lost one game.

Not that he'd seen one. Trace rarely had time to do more than grab a box of doughnuts. The early morning call, while robbing him of sleep, allowed a longer stop at the Sugar Shack for friendship and plenty of Miriam's rich-roast coffee.

He took a long, noisy sip.

"You and Cheyenne enjoy the movie last night?"

Oh. This was about Cheyenne. After the night on the bridge, their relationship *had* shifted. Though neither voiced the change, he no longer had to use after-hours calls as an excuse to be with her. He asked. She accepted.

She'd even begun attending Kitty's Bible study, a move that caused a veritable symphony in his spirit.

"She understands the well now," he said simply, partly to share the good news and partly to deflect the question.

Popbottle Jones, who had been deep in conversation at another table, returned, carrying a brown paper sack filled with 8-track tapes. Trace didn't even know the things existed anymore. Knowing Popbottle Jones and G. I. Jack, they'd concoct some use for the outdated recordings and probably make money in the deal.

"She stopped by the house one day." Popbottle turned to G. I. Jack. "Saturday evening, wasn't it?"

"Seems to be my recollection, though my memory ain't what she once was."

The fact that Cheyenne had visited the two old gentlemen came as a surprise to Trace. She hadn't said a word.

"I believe she's on the mend, Doc." The dignified old man, dressed in his ever-present suit of castoffs—this one of olive worsted—nodded sagely. "Did she mention how her Saturday afternoon library circle has grown by yet another woman?"

Trace was impressed with the library circle, as Cheyenne called the weekly meeting of abused women. Though Emma remained in the home with Ray, she was studying for her GED at the library, a class Cheyenne had arranged. Maybe someday she'd stand on her own two feet. Cheyenne was ecstatic with her progress. He was ecstatic with Cheyenne, though he was afraid to let that bit of news out on the wind just yet.

He still worried about her and the other woman, given the husband's predilection for rage. So far, nothing volatile had occurred. He hoped the peace lasted.

"She has. I understand I have you to thank for the latest addition."

"Favor Lee's been down the road of domestic violence and come out on the other side, stronger and better. We figured her experience would give the other women encouragement that they, too, can be happy and safe again."

Cheyenne's little group now consisted of five, including herself. And she was badgering the Chamber and the Town Council and anyone else who would listen to investigate the feasibility of opening a shelter in Redemption.

He had a sudden memory of her eyes, darker than Miriam's espresso, as she spoke of her plans. She wanted to make a difference. Trace had no doubt she would.

"She's amazing," he said.

Popbottle Jones arched one bushy white eyebrow. "I didn't realize you knew Favor Lee that well."

Heat crept up Trace's neck and burned in his ears. The two old dudes burst out laughing.

"I told you so," G. I. Jack guffawed. "You got the look."

Might as well ask. He set his coffee cup carefully onto the saucer. "Exactly what kind of look, G.I.?"

The old man slipped a biscuit into his pocket and, with a grin bigger than a melon slice, said, "Love, boy. You got the look of a man in love."

• • •

She was healed. Set free. Alive again.

"Like this, Cheyenne?" Zoey's small fingers trilled the treble clef notes while Cheyenne added a simplified bass rhythm.

"You got it, doll face."

For three weeks now, Cheyenne had not had a nightmare or a flashback. Not since the night she'd prayed and really believed that God loved her enough to give her a restful sleep—with the lights out.

God loved her. She could hardly take it in. Trace and Kitty claimed He loved everyone no matter what.

Of course, they didn't know the worst about her. But God knew.

Since that night, she'd slept, she'd worked, she'd gotten involved in Redemption's city politics in an attempt to help battered women, an act that had scared her silly at first. What if the cops ran a background check? But why would they? And if they did, so what? She'd done nothing illegal. Ethically as well as legally, the cops could not discuss her private life.

The only fly in her hopeful ointment was Trace Bowman and this incredibly precious little girl, Zoey.

She'd been less than truthful on that front, but like the moth drawn to the flame, she went right on spending time with him. At first, the piano lessons had been an excuse to stay longer, have dinner, watch TV, take a walk. But now neither of them bothered with excuses.

Sunday he'd invited her to church . . . and she'd gone. That alone gave her a new excuse. Trace was a missionary masquerading as a veterinarian. She was his latest project for God. Her brother said she was asking for trouble. Kitty claimed God was trying to bless her. And her interesting new friends, G. I. Jack and Popbottle Jones, did nothing but extol Trace's virtues—which was completely unnecessary. She already knew the man was a cross between Pollyanna, some holy saint and the best-looking movie star in Hollywood.

Abruptly, Zoey stopped playing, leaving the birthday song dangling in the air. "Am I, Cheyenne?"

Cheyenne rested her left hand on the keyboard. "Are you what?"

"A doll face? What does my face look like?"

The child had a way of getting right to the heart of matters and touching Cheyenne to the core. Love splashed in the center of Cheyenne's being and sent concentric waves of joy flowing through her.

"You're very beautiful, Zoey. I'm sure your friends have told you."

"Yes, but I want to know what you think."

"Now you know," she said softly as she traced

a finger around Zoey's hairline, outlining her cheek and jaw and forehead. "You have an oval face, a special shape associated with beauty. Your mouth curves upward so you look happy all the time."

"That's because I am happy."

"And your nose is perfect. Not too long, not too short."

"What about my eyes? Are they weird?"

Cheyenne swallowed. "No."

"Jeremy Pilson said they were. He said I look creepy because my eyes don't go anywhere."

The cruel bluntness of children. Cheyenne ached for the little girl. "Your eyes are blue like your daddy's. A beautiful dark blue surrounded by very black eyelashes. They beam with an inner light so powerful, women around the world envy eyes such as yours."

She ended the description with a tap on the nose and a quick hug. Zoey clung to her for a second longer before sitting back.

"What do *you* look like, Cheyenne? Daddy says you're really, really pretty. He gets a funny sound in his voice when he talks about you. Can I touch your face and see with my fingers?"

Daddy said that? He gets a funny sound in his voice. What did that mean?

"Sure." She remained still while Zoey explored, wiggling her nose once because the light skim of fingers tickled.

Zoey laughed. "You're ticklish."

"Feels like spiders crawling on my face."

This delighted the little girl. She tickled some more and Cheyenne responded with exaggerated facial gyrations beneath the curious fingers that brought more giggles. Soon, an all-out tickle fest ensued.

When the giggles ended, Zoey threw her arms around Cheyenne and clung like Saran Wrap. "I love you, Cheyenne."

What else could she say but the truth? "I love you, too, doll face."

Twice a week Trace entered his living room to this same sight. And yet his heart never adjusted. The foolish muscle skittered, stumbled, regrouped and pounded like bongos.

Zoey and Cheyenne seated at the piano, long black hair flowing down both their backs, took his breath away. Once, he'd compared Cheyenne to Pamela. No more. Now his stomach lifted along with his spirits to know Cheyenne would be waiting when he arrived, nurturing his daughter as her mother would have. Pamela would not only approve; she would be grateful. As he was.

He paused in the doorway to observe as he often did, letting the sight fill him to the brim.

"Color is like music," Cheyenne was saying.

"How?" Zoey's pretty face tilted toward her

teacher. "Like brown is chocolate pudding?"

"Sort of. Take green for instance. Green is cool, relaxing and calming. Green is the smell of a fresh mowed lawn and the sound of water flowing over the rocks in spring. Listen. This is green." Cheyenne's fingers moved over the ivories in a graceful, flowing motion as she played a soothing tune that did indeed remind him of green pastures and calming waters.

He closed his eyes, letting the music sweep over him, along with G. I. Jack's words. The old gent was right. He loved Cheyenne Rhodes. If he hadn't loved her before, he loved her now. She was the other half of him that had been missing for eight years.

Thank You, God, for another chance to love. Don't let me mess this up.

When the gentle sweep of music finished, Zoey's face lit up, enraptured. "Wait until I tell Daddy."

Trace's breath clogged in his throat. He cleared away the thick emotion. "I leave you two alone for an hour and look what happens."

Both females swiveled toward him. Zoey slid off the piano bench, one arm extended, and came in his direction. "Daddy! I know green."

He swooped her up. "I heard. Pretty impressive."

His gaze sought out Cheyenne. She was smiling gently, her love for Zoey as obvious as God's

243

love for them all. She loved his child. Did she love him, too? Everything inside him said she did.

As Zoey skipped away to call her best friend with the glorious news about musical color, Trace decided then and there. He loved Cheyenne Rhodes. He wanted her in his life. And there was no time like the present.

The expression on Trace's face brought a tremor to Cheyenne as he came toward her, hands out-stretched. As if connected by an invisible cord, she rose from the piano bench and twined her fingers with his.

"You're amazing," he said as he pulled her close and kissed the hair above her ear. She shivered with the pure beauty of being in Trace's arms again. Not since the night on the river bridge had he held or kissed her, other than holding her hand on walks.

"How was the patient?" she murmured.

"Fine. Forget the patient." His tone was gruff and manly, a combination that sent a surprising thrill down her spine. "I want to talk about us."

"Us?" She heard the squeak in her voice.

With exquisite care, Trace threaded his fingers along her jawline and into her hair, cupping her chin with the heels of his hands. Eye to eye and heart to heart, his lips grazed hers, his breath warm and minty.

"I love you, Cheyenne."

"Oh, Trace."

A quizzical curve lifted the corner of his mouth. "That's all? Just, oh, Trace?"

Running her fingertips along his jaw, she smiled into eyes dark with emotion. Every fiber of her being yearned toward this good, good man. Did she dare take a chance?

A sudden realization slammed into her like the recoil of a .44 mag, only without the giant bloody mess. She loved Trace Bowman. Really, really loved him. Not the adolescent, self-seeking emotion she'd felt for Paul. The kind of love that not only wanted to laugh at his jokes and work beside him in the clinic, but the kind that wanted to understand his dark places, soothe his hurts and make his life better. She wanted to make his life perfect and good and beautiful.

Please, God, let this be right.

"You're the finest man I've ever known. And—" she drew on every last ounce of courage "—I love you, too."

The relief and joy in his expression melted her.

"I want you in my life. With me and Zoey. Forever. How does that sound to you?"

Perfect. Absolutely perfect.

"Good."

The word was muffled by the sweetness of his lips. She quivered like Jell-O, yearning to be everything he needed, to bring him happiness the way he'd done for her.

The old doubts surfaced, threatening and reminding. He didn't know everything. Would he still love her then?

But she was healed. The past was behind her. She was no longer a basket case ready to go off the deep end at any moment.

Some things were better left unsaid.

Weren't they?

"I want to show you something," he said, gently breaking their embrace.

Bemused, happy, she responded, "What is it?"

"A surprise." He tugged her hand. "Come on."

"What about dinner?"

His dimples flashed. "Dinner? Woman, I've waited for you for eight years. Dinner can wait a while."

Laughing, breathless and more lighthearted than she could remember being in a long time, Cheyenne let him lead the way. Whatever the surprise, she would love it because she loved him.

He led her past the living room, through the kitchen and into the utility room that opened into the garage.

No big deal. She'd been inside his garage a couple of times.

In broad daylight. With the big door open to the outside.

"My great-grandpa gave this to my great-grandma as a betrothal gift," Trace was saying. He opened the door leading into the garage. Her muscles tensed. The breathlessness became exaggerated.

Trace stepped down inside, but Cheyenne hesitated on the threshold, staring into the dark confines. One glimpse toward the end told her the door was closed.

She'd managed to avoid a closed garage since that hideous night when she'd had a flashback in front of Trace.

Oblivious to her distress Trace opened a storage room. "After her dad agreed to let them marry, Great-Grandpa cranked this victrola and serenaded his bride-to-be."

He pulled away some kind of cover to reveal an antique record player, but Cheyenne couldn't focus.

Tightness squeezed at her throat. She swallowed hard.

She could always ask him to press the garage-door opener first.

But he would ask questions.

Besides, there was no need to open the door. She was over all that. This was Trace's garage and she was with Trace, the man she loved.

The man she loved.

"I love you," she whispered, putting one foot on the first of two steps down into the garage.

"I even have the old record they danced to." He turned, holding out his arms. "Will you celebrate with me the way my grand—Hey, you're shaking!"

Cheyenne paused, trying not to let her anxiety show. Trace studied her, and his bewilderment slowly turned to comprehension. His arms fell to his sides. "Wait, I'll open the door."

But it was too late; she'd stepped into the darkened space and though the light overhead flickered on, Trace began to fade. In seconds, she no longer saw the man she loved.

She saw Dwight Hector.

"No." She stumbled back, one hand flung up in defense. "Back off. I have a gun."

The clawing in her brain accelerated. Thrust back in time, she relived the smell and terror and pain.

She fought the feeling, telling herself to snap out of it. This was a flashback. The attack was not really happening. Dwight Hector was dead.

Some part of her understood. Another part refused to listen.

Arms, far too strong to defeat, wrapped around her.

"Cheyenne." He shook her. "Cheyenne."

She fought and kicked but could not escape. Whimpering now, helpless and hopeless, she collapsed on the cold cement floor and let him do the unthinkable.

"Cheyenne, sweetheart, you're okay. I'm sorry. I forgot about the claustrophobia. I'm so sorry. Please, you're scaring me to death. Come back to me."

Fighting the dreadful undertow of terror, Cheyenne leaned toward the frightened voice. Trace?

Slowly, the fog began to lift.

"Look at me. Open your eyes and look at me." A gentle hand raised her chin.

She didn't want to see a dead man's face. But the voice didn't belong to Hector. This was Trace.

"Trace?"

Struggling harder, determined to regain control, she forced her eyelids up.

The concern and fear in Trace's expression shattered her.

She was huddled on the floor of the garage, knees drawn up tight to her chin. Trace held her from the side, shaking more than a little. If her heart hadn't already been broken, that would have done it.

"I thought I was healed," she whispered, throat ragged and raw.

But she wasn't healed. She would never be. Whatever peace she'd found in this town and in Kitty's book had only been a temporary reprieve.

"You are. You will be. We'll get through this.

Whatever the problem is, we'll get through it together."

With her heart splintering into a million pieces, she pulled away from his wonderful embrace, straightened her trembling legs and stood.

"No." She shook her head.

He stepped toward her but she backed away. "No. I'm sorry. This won't work."

"What are you saying? What won't work?"

She shook her head again. "Us. We won't work, Trace. I need to go."

"No way you're leaving like this." He gripped her shoulders.

"Don't touch me." Her voice rose. She jerked away.

His expression stricken, his hands fell to his sides.

She clamped her eyes shut against the pain in his face. He didn't deserve to go through this. He didn't deserve a damaged woman with more baggage than the airport.

"Talk to me, Cheyenne. Trust me. With God's help, we can work through this."

The hurt sliding over his handsome features threatened to bring her to her knees. Of all the stupid things she'd done in the past year, getting involved with the town vet ranked at the top.

"There's nothing to work out. I don't—" She drew in a breath of musty, garage-scented air. "I don't want to work things out."

The lie tore through her heart like a flaming arrow.

"What are you talking about? You love me."

How could she deny such a beautiful thing?

"Love isn't enough." And with deep sorrow, she knew the words were true. She loved Trace and Zoey too much to saddle them with her.

The only way she could make life better for the two that held her heart was to leave them alone. As badly as she wanted, she couldn't be the woman they needed.

The hardest thing she'd ever had to do happened in that moment. Harder than hearing her life and mistakes played out in the media, harder than testifying in court. Harder even than enduring a brutal rape.

She walked out of Trace's garage—and his life—and didn't look back.

Chapter Fifteen

෴

Over the next couple of days Trace wandered around in a fog. He went through the motions, treated patients, responded to friends and employees, but inside he was shell-shocked.

He still couldn't understand what had happened

that night. One minute, Cheyenne declared her love and the next she'd walked out. Other than a voice message on the office machine tendering her resignation effectively immediately, he hadn't been able to make contact. All his phone calls went unanswered. He'd driven by the motel a couple of times, too, but if she'd been home, she'd pretended otherwise.

He'd even stooped to telephoning Kitty, but all the motel proprietor could tell him was that Cheyenne seemed okay. How could she be okay when he was destroyed?

She wasn't okay. He knew as surely as he knew the precise dosage of rabies vaccine. Something was deeply wrong in Cheyenne's world and if she would only let him in, with God's help, they could fix it.

Usually, he loved his job but today the stream of dogs and cats had seemed endless. Add to that the stares and concerned glances of his employees, their whispers when they thought he wasn't listening, and he'd been ready to throw up his hands and quit.

He had been relieved when the day was finally over.

With a weary sigh, he collapsed on the sofa, and rubbed work-roughened hands over his face.

Soft footfalls stirred the carpet.

"Want to talk about it, son?"

"No point."

"Sometimes talking helps to clear the air." His mother perched next to him, a comforting hand on his knee. "I've noticed Cheyenne hasn't been around the past day or two."

He kept his burning eyes focused on the speckled beige pattern in the carpet. "No."

"Is she the problem?"

Hesitating, he heaved a sigh. "Yes."

Mom was a nurturer. She'd have to fight the need to rush in and make things right, but telling her eased the band of pain around his chest.

"Dad and I could tell you were falling for her." Mom's voice was soft, compassionate. *Thank You, God, for a great mother.*

"Hard."

"Because she reminded you of Pamela?"

"Maybe at first, but not now." He sat back, rolling his head toward her. "I love you, Mom. Thanks for caring. I just need some time, okay?"

This wasn't a knee scrape she could kiss.

She patted his leg and rose. "You know where we are if you need us, honey. Don't brood too long. The Lord has a plan and purpose. Keep looking."

Body heavy with fatigue and emotion, he followed her to the door, kissed her cheek and watched her drive away, leaving behind her love and lasagna.

"Daddy?" Zoey's voice sounded small and worried behind him. "Is Cheyenne mad at us?"

Slowly, he closed the door, waited for the latch to click before responding. "No one could be mad at you, pumpkin."

"But she didn't come today. And I heard what Grandma said. I thought maybe she was mad at us."

How did he explain the complexities of adult relationships to a second grader? He hunkered in front of her, hands on her soft, slender arms. She was like fairy dust, fragile and tender and utterly beautiful. All that he was as a man and a father existed to protect his special child from hurt.

"She's not mad. Cheyenne is sad. We have to pray for her."

Zoey's sensitive, brilliant fingers found his cheeks. "You're sad, too."

"Yes."

"Is she never, ever coming back?"

"I don't think so."

"But she works for you. She still comes to the clinic, doesn't she?"

He shook his head, aware that another heart, other than his, was aching. "She quit."

"Did you say something mean to her?"

To his recollection, a declaration of love was not mean. There was no way he would discuss Cheyenne's panic attack. Zoey would be terrified.

"No, Zoey. I'd never do that."

"I know you wouldn't, Daddy." She patted his cheeks. "You're too nice."

"Yeah." And nice guys finish last.

He was not usually into self-pity, but today he'd euthanized a family's suffering Labrador retriever and then hadn't been able to save a rancher's mare. The colic had gone too far before he'd arrived, but still he blamed himself. Bad day all the way around.

"I love her, Daddy." Zoey moved in, clung to his neck, her head against his shoulder. "I thought she loved us, too. I want her to be my mommy."

He nearly choked on the admission. "She does love us, pumpkin. I'm sure of it." But according to Cheyenne, love wasn't enough. "We have to pray real hard for Cheyenne. She's sad inside about something."

"About what?"

"I wish I knew, but she won't tell me. She thinks she's bad for us." He stroked a hand down the cascade of silk hair so like Cheyenne's.

"But she's not. She taught me colors and piano and she started learning Braille, so we could read together."

Trace squeezed his eyes tight. He hadn't known about the Braille.

Zoey's head came up. "I have an idea, Daddy."

"And what might that be?"

"Let's go get Cheyenne and fix her. We'll tell her how much we love her and tell her she never has to be sad anymore. You can give her one of the puppies and buy her presents, and we'll all live together and be happy. Okay?"

If life were only that simple.

"Let me explain something." He shifted her around onto one thigh. "The Bible says God has a perfect plan for your life and for mine."

"And Cheyenne's?"

His eyes dropped shut while he prayed for guidance. Whatever he said now could influence Zoey's attitude toward God forever. "Yes, baby. Cheyenne's, too."

She sighed, her face a wreath of confusion.

He tried again. "You know God loves you, right?"

"Yep. More than you do. More than chocolate chip cookies or baby puppies."

Those were two of Zoey's most loved things. He smiled, though the motion was filled with sadness. "Right. He loves you so much He wants the very, very best for your life."

"Cheyenne is the best."

Lord, help me.

"Someday, when God is ready, He will send the right mommy for you and the right wife for Daddy." He hoped he wasn't lying to his child. "But until then, we have to be patient and wait for His perfect timing."

A huge tear leaked from the corner of Zoey's sightless eyes. "But I don't want a perfect timing. I want Cheyenne."

Staring across his living room to the silent piano, Trace pulled Zoey against his chest and held her.

What more could he say? He wanted Cheyenne, too.

"Sorry, hon, I hired someone yesterday. Must have forgot to take down that sign."

The woman whipped around the counter of the Charity Lane Git-and-Go Convenience Store and ripped the cellophane-taped poster from the window.

Cheyenne's shoulders drooped. This was the fourth help-wanted sign so far today that had "accidently" been left in a window.

"If you hear of anything else—" she started.

The woman paused and cocked one hip. "Listen, sweetie, why don't you go on back out to Doc Bowman's? I hear he could sure use your help. And that Zoey child misses you something awful."

Bringing Zoey into the equation was a low blow. She was already suffering enormous guilt in that department. She wanted to talk to the child, to explain . . . something. Maybe she'd call her after school before Trace arrived home. But what could she possibly say that would make any difference? What could she say that wouldn't make things worse?

"Thank you, anyway," she said, and left the store.

This exasperating, endearing bunch of towns-people clearly adored their vet and his daughter. And they were not going to give up easily.

She missed Zoey and Trace something terrible, but her feelings didn't matter. She'd made the right choice for them. They might not understand that, but she did.

She glanced down at the weekly newspaper lying open on the car seat. Most of the ads were outdated by now, but she might as well check them out. Jobless was not an option. Find work or move on to a larger town.

Perhaps that was the best idea. Hit the road. Move on. Keep running. Don't look back.

The very idea stole her breath.

But she had to consider leaving town as a valid option.

"Cashion's Laundromat and Car Wash," she muttered, and clung to the fading prospect that someone in Redemption wasn't a born match-maker. If life had any compassion at all, that particular person would own and operate the local pink laundry.

Winding past downtown, she spotted the Town Square. Something pulled at her. She'd not been back to the pretty park since the night Trace had brought her.

Parking parallel, she hopped out of the car and crossed the street to enter the square. The flowers in bloom had changed since her first visit. Yellow and red cannas now swayed like stately ladies beside the pathways. Fresh grass clippings scattered along the concrete shot green smells into the air and warned of the lawn mower ahead. Sure enough, two city employees were hard at work, grooming the square.

A pair of teenagers sat on one bench, iPod buds crammed in their ears while eating carry-out. On another, a young mother and two children fed bread crumbs to two brown squirrels. Both animals sat upright like tiny, endearing children, begging for bread.

Cheyenne passed them by with a smile and a nod. She'd learned to do that in Redemption, to say hello to perfect strangers. As Zoey said, "A stranger is just a friend you've never met before."

Her heart crimped.

Zoey. Precious Zoey.

What would it hurt to stop by and say hello? Maybe offer piano lessons again after school?

No, that was asking for trouble.

Approaching the well, she went directly to the plaque and read the inscription. For a while, she'd believed the words, but now she was right back where she'd started. Well, maybe she wasn't as tormented and angry, but she was every bit as broken. Only this time for a different reason.

"Kinda makes a body feel good, don't it?"

At the intrusive voice, Cheyenne startled, turning to find Popbottle Jones and G. I. Jack standing right behind her.

"I didn't hear you walk up," she said, amazed not to have slapped her side for a weapon. Amazed even more not to have been frightened. Maybe she had changed more than she thought.

"Pardon the surprise attack but we were perusing the municipal bins for untapped treasures and witnessed your arrival."

G. I. Jack's grizzled gray head bobbed. "Yep. And we been wanting to talk to you."

"Really?" Her defenses shot up. "About what?" As if she couldn't guess.

"Well, why don't you humor two pitiful old men and give us a few minutes of your time?"

These old codgers were anything but pitiful, but they'd been kindness personified. How could she refuse?

"All right." Stiffly, she followed them to a bench and perched. G.I. and Popbottle settled in, one on either side.

"How you been doing, Cheyenne?" G. I. Jack removed a handful of discarded pop tops from his pocket along with a Boy Scout knife and a thin cord of some type.

"All right, I guess. Jobs are hard to find in this town."

"Well, you see, my dear, that is precisely what

260

we wished to speak with you about. You are not in need of a job."

She clenched her jaw. If he told her she had a job with Trace, she'd scream. "Yes, I am."

"No, my dear. What you need is a heart transplant."

"A what?" she asked, laughing at Popbottle's ridiculous statement.

G. I. Jack bobbed as Popbottle Jones went on talking. "Each of us suffers difficulty in this life. That's the nature of the universe. None of us gets through unscathed. A pity, but factual nonetheless." His dignified old head pivoted toward her. Green eyes pierced her as though they knew her secrets. With a sinking realization, she figured they did. "But the Lord Almighty with His vast and generous love makes a way to escape."

"That's Bible right there, Miss Cheyenne." G. I. Jack twisted and snipped at the pop tops, a worthless mess of metal, if you asked her. "Corinthians, I believe."

"Indeed. The Lord offers us a heart transplant, a chance to make all things new again. He can take something broken and worthless and make it beautiful."

She scoffed. "Impossible."

Both men stiffened. G. I. Jack's fingers paused in cutting a bit of the cord.

"We are speaking of God Almighty," Popbottle said. "Creator of the universe."

Properly chastised, Cheyenne clapped her mouth shut. Let the old dudes speak their piece. Even if she disagreed with their theology, they meânt well.

"Your soul has been battered and your heart emptied, but the Lord has sent a fine man and a very special child to fill it up again."

Staring at the close-clipped grass, she said, "You don't understand the situation."

"I think we do. But let me ask you a question. Is it better to live in the light but to be filled with inner darkness and fear? Or to be like Zoey, who lives in darkness and yet she is full of light and has no fear?"

"That's not a fair question." Zoey was a child. She'd never seen the ugly side of life.

An arrow pierced her conscience. Zoey would never see anything.

"Oh, but the question *is* fair, Cheyenne."

"Yep. Sure is. God is light." G. I. Jack looked up from his work, but his thick, shockingly agile fingers never stopped working. Sun glinted on the metal pieces. "That's what the Good Book says. If we have Him, we have the light."

"But I've prayed and I read Kitty's devotional. The nightmares went away and I was doing better. I thought the worst was over and then—" She caught her bottom lip between her teeth, shutting off the flow of words before she revealed too much. "It's not fair to Trace and Zoey."

"Some healings take more time."

"Sometimes we need other folks to help us get there. Trace is good folks."

Both men stood as if the conversation was over. G. I. Jack unfolded her clenched fist and dropped the metal pieces inside before reclosing her fingers. Then the pair ambled off across the green flowered square, past the fountain and across the street.

Deep inside, she knew they were right. Her wounds were more than physical and emotional; they were dark places in her soul. Until she exposed them to light and love, she would never completely heal.

She opened her hand and looked down at G.I.'s gift. The worthless, broken pop tops had been transformed into a beautiful bracelet of silver butterflies.

Emma arrived at ten that night.

"Can I stay with you until the morning?" she asked when Cheyenne opened the door.

Cheyenne glanced around outside. The darkness pulsed with summer life—car noises, door slams, a dog's bark. "Come inside and we'll talk."

Once the door was safely shut, Cheyenne asked, "What happened?"

"The same old stuff. Only this time I decided to get out before he exploded."

"Smart. But I'm not sure staying here is the best idea."

Emma's thin face twitched with uncertainty. "I don't know where else to go."

If only Redemption would embrace her idea of a shelter.

"Okay, let me think a minute. Maybe Kitty has another unit available."

"I don't want to be by myself."

She had a good point. "Then I could stay with you, but I think Ray is likely to come to the motel first. You've been here before."

"But not for a long time. And I don't think he suspects about the library meetings."

"Let me call Kitty. She should still be awake."

As Cheyenne reached for the telephone, the sound of car tires churning gravel caught her ear. A door slammed, prickling the hair on her scalp. Exchanging glances with Emma, she put the receiver down and started to the window.

Ray Madden kicked in her door.

Chapter Sixteen

୨

Trace was restless as a housefly. He stalked from one room to the next, flipped the TV off and on, ate a piece of his mom's cherry cake he didn't want and even began to wish for an emergency call.

With Zoey spending the night at Grandma's, his mind was where it seemed to be too often—on Cheyenne.

He rubbed a hand over the back of his neck. Three days seemed like an eternity without talking to her. Was she okay? G. I. Jack and Popbottle Jones had dropped by the clinic this afternoon with not-so-subtle hints that he should talk to Cheyenne "one more time."

He'd been thinking about that.

Time to act instead of thinking. He grabbed his truck keys and hustled out the door.

"Get out of my apartment." Without taking her eyes off the enraged man, Cheyenne said quietly, "Emma, call the police."

She stood between Ray Madden and his wife, shaking on the inside but mad as a nest of hornets on the outside. Emma seemed nailed to the floor, too pale and scared to move.

As if Cheyenne wasn't in the room, Ray Madden started toward his wife.

Cheyenne grabbed his arm. The muscle was hard as cast iron. No wonder Emma was afraid of his fists. He paused, glaring a hole through her. "Back off."

He spat a curse. Cheyenne curled her lip. Whoopee, the big bad boy knew a big bad word. She was so impressed.

"Sorry, dude. Not going to happen. In case you didn't notice, that was my front door you busted."

"Not the only thing I'm going to bust." He growled the threatening words.

"Just go, Ray," Emma pleaded, voice trembling, face as white as paste. "I'm staying."

"Don't be stupid. Get in the car now if you know what's good for you."

Except for her obvious trembling, Emma didn't move. For once, she stood her ground. Ray's nostrils flared. His eyes bulged. Fury rippled off him in waves. Any minute now and he would blow. Sure as she'd worked these scenes dozens of times, Cheyenne knew.

"Why don't we do this the easy way, Ray?" she murmured. Sometimes the calm approach worked. Most times, not.

Swinging his massive forearm, the man shoved at Cheyenne. She stumbled back, caught her hip painfully on the edge of a table but didn't give in.

"Mr. Madden, you need to calm down a minute and let's discuss this like adults." She shot another quick glance at Emma. "Call 9-1-1."

Ray glared as if she was crazy. Maybe she was. But he wasn't taking Emma, nor was he going to hurt her. No other woman would suffer at the hands of a man if Cheyenne Rhodes had any say in the matter.

"No discussion," he said. "She goes home with me. Emma, move now, or I swear—"

Cheyenne shoved a chair up beside him. "Why don't you sit down first?"

He kicked it. The chair flipped over, thudding against the carpet.

With the front door splintered and a clear shot into the living area, Cheyenne hoped someone nearby would notice and sound the alarm. Emma seemed too frightened to make the call, and Cheyenne couldn't get to the phone. The Glock was in her purse, out of reach. Just like before.

She squelched the aberrant thought. This was nothing like before.

"Please, Ray," Emma whispered. She'd backed against the wall, near the bathroom. Why hadn't the woman grabbed the telephone first? "Just go home and get some sleep. We'll talk tomorrow."

Go in the bathroom and lock the door.

Cheyenne tried to signal with her eyes, but the message was lost when Ray thrust her to the side and dove toward Emma. Cheyenne fell across the bed. Emma's scream ripped through the night.

God, if You're listening, let someone hear her scream. Show me what to do.

Clawing up from the rumple of covers and pillows, she stood on wobbly legs.

Ray had Emma pressed against the wall. The terror in the other woman's face was too much to bear.

With no regard for herself, she threw herself between Ray's raised fist and Emma's face. He struck Cheyenne's shoulder. Throwing her arm up to ward off another blow, she kicked for his shin.

The blow enraged him more.

Cheyenne's hair hung loose and he grabbed a handful, shaking her like a rag doll. Her teeth rattled. Her ears rang, but she fought back, jabbing her fist beneath his chin. He grunted.

In the melee, Emma had slithered to the floor and crawled away. From the corner of her eye, Cheyenne saw her go for the phone. It was too late for that. He'd be on her in a blink.

"Run. Get help. *Go!*"

As if survival instinct had finally kicked in, Emma bolted from the room, leaving Cheyenne alone. Alone with a raging maniac. Again.

• • •

Trace slowed the truck as he approached the motel and turned into the space next to Cheyenne's car. His truck lights slid over her apartment.

What he saw froze the blood in his veins. The front door stood open, the wood splintered into pieces. Emma Madden darted from the apartment, screaming.

Adrenaline jacked into Trace's bloodstream at Mach speed. He was out of the truck and had hold of Emma's arm before his brain connected the dots. "Where's Cheyenne?"

"Ray, he—" She pointed at the splintered door.

Her expression raised the hairs on the back of his neck. "Call the police."

He hit the door running.

A man twice her size gripped Cheyenne's long, beautiful hair while she swung and kicked and dodged his other hand. With his superior strength and rage, there was no way she could ward him off much longer.

Trace Bowman was a peace-loving man, but he'd wrestled his fair share of mad bulls and wild stallions. Ray Madden was only a man.

He tapped the massive shoulder. "Hey, buddy. Wanna fight?"

Before Madden could react, Trace wrapped a biceps around the man's neck and yanked in, hard and tight. Madden went down like an anesthetized horse. The floor thundered with his landing.

"Trace. Oh, thank God. Trace." Cheyenne launched herself into his arms, trembling like a drowned kitten.

He nearly crumbled. "You okay? Where are you hurt? Let me see."

With a groan he buried his face in her tangled, matted hair. Oh, her beautiful hair. He was tempted to stomp his boot on Ray Madden's unconscious nose.

"Trace," Cheyenne said again as though his name was the only word that mattered.

"You're okay. I'm here, tough girl. You done good."

She snuggled into him and let him hold her.

He could deal with that.

Sirens wailed nearby. Blue and white lights strobed the living room. Doors slammed, voices called and footsteps crunched the gravel outside.

Suddenly the room was filled with people. Cops, paramedics, Kitty and Emma, neighbors.

"Is Cheyenne okay?" Kitty, in a white robe and furry blue slippers, stood with an arm around Emma's shoulders.

Trace couldn't bear to loosen his hold long enough to look. He never wanted to let her go again. But paramedics insisted.

"Better let us check her over, Doc."

270

Cheyenne came to life then. "I'm okay. Just get him out of here." She shot a disgusted glance at the now conscious and clearly befuddled attacker. "Book him. Domestic abuse, breaking and entering, assault and battery. And, yes, I most definitely will press charges."

The cop in charge lifted an eyebrow. "Anything else?"

"I'm still thinking."

Trace held back a laugh. She was mad. Good. That meant she'd recover.

She quickly filled the officers in on the situation, using precise coplike terms that had them all gazing at her with comical expressions. Emma spoke, too, though her remarks were given with a constant eye to her now-docile husband. Head down, handcuffed and defeated, he was a sad sight. Trace could almost feel sympathy for a man cursed by alcohol and jealousy.

But one glance at Cheyenne and the red mark on her cheek, the tangle of black hair and the barely concealed fear in her espresso eyes stirred the fire in his blood again.

Gently, he touched the spot on her cheek. She winced.

"Sure you're not hurt?"

"No. How did you—?"

She stopped talking as Madden was hauled out of the building, trailed by the emergency crews. A visible shudder passed through her body. Trace

271

couldn't help himself. He had to hold her again.

"I'm taking Emma to my place for the night." Kitty appeared in his line of vision. "You'll take care of Cheyenne?"

"Count on it."

If Cheyenne had objections she didn't say so. Too bad if she did. He was here. He was staying, even if that meant sitting outside on the porch until dawn with his back against this shattered door. A man didn't come this close to losing his woman without taking the matter personally.

Kitty's mouth curved in a knowing smile. She handed Trace a key. "She can stay in the next room. I'll call Jace and get him to fix the door tomorrow. Ya'll take care now. Good night."

Cheyenne rallied then. "Wait."

The other two women turned as Cheyenne walked over and spoke to the shivering Emma. "None of this was your fault, Emma. This was his choice, not yours. Ray made the decision to be violent. He made the decision to bust in here. Not you. You have a right to be safe. You have a right to live free from fear. Promise me you will remember that."

Emma, arms crossed protectively over her pink T-shirt, nodded. Moistening her lips, she whispered, "I remember everything you've told me. If not for you—"

Cheyenne cut her off with a quick hug. "Go on now. Get some rest. You are going to make it."

Trace's chest swelled with pride. This was his Cheyenne in action. No wonder he was crazy about her.

With gratitude, he watched the widow and Emma step over the busted door and disappear into the darkness.

The noise in Cheyenne's apartment subsided to a stunned silence, broken only by the traffic noise clearly heard through the shattered door.

When Cheyenne turned back, Trace could no more resist the need to keep her close than he could give birth. He reached for her.

"We have to talk," she said.

He drew her to his chest, pleased when she came willingly, easily as though she needed his touch as much as he needed hers. After tonight, he never wanted her out of his sight again.

"I'd rather hold you."

Her lips curved against his neck. "Talk first. Hold later."

Did that mean—? He relinquished his grip and gazed down at her. "I'm going to hold you to that."

"Ha-ha. Punny." Her smile, though wan, was genuine. They were gaining ground. "I have to tell you something very important."

He could tell he wasn't going to like it. "Okay."

"But first, how did you do that? How did you take Madden down so easily?"

"Rear-naked choke hold."

"I recognized the sleeper hold. How did you know how to do it?"

"High school wrestling team. Never used the maneuver, but always wanted to."

He thought she might laugh. "Doc, I didn't know you had such aggression in you."

"I have a lot in me when it comes to protecting someone I love."

The tension around her eyes softened. She stroked his jaw. "Incredible man. What am I going to do about you?"

"Love me? Trust me? Let me inside that gorgeous head of yours."

She bit down on her bottom lip. His belly flip-flopped.

"I want to."

"That's a start."

"I talked with G. I. Jack and Popbottle Jones earlier. They had some advice. There are things you need to know about me. Bad things."

"Nothing can change who you are to me. Don't you get that yet? The Cheyenne I know is strong and incredibly brave, loving and good."

Tears glimmered, unshed in her dark eyes. "Not good. I'm not good, Trace."

"I don't know who told you that, but I may have to use the sleeper hold on them, too." He tugged at her. "Come on. Sit down and let's clear the air. My knees are shaking."

"Mine, too."

After righting the upturned chair, they both were seated at the small round dining table. Trace folded his arms on the tabletop and leaned toward her. "Talk."

The scared look leaped into her face.

"Don't do that. Whatever you have to say, I'm ready to hear it." He hoped he wasn't lying. But he knew she couldn't embrace the future until something in her past was laid to rest.

"Something happened in Colorado. About a year ago."

"I figured as much. Does this have anything to do with the guy you shot in the line of duty?"

"Yes." She swallowed, then cupped her fingers around her mouth, inhaling deeply as if gathering all the courage in the room.

Dread began to form in his belly. He knew beyond a doubt that he was about to hear something he would hate.

Lord, let me be what she needs. And give her the strength she needs to get past this, whatever it is. Heal her spirit. I love her, God. I love her.

As if reciting a story she'd relived hundreds of times, Cheyenne began to speak in a low, controlled, emotionless tone.

"I was assigned to a special task force to track down a—" She looked down.

Trace laid his hand over her fidgeting ones. "A what, honey?"

275

Her gaze flashed up and then away again. "A rapist."

A shock of ice went down his spine. He held his breath, afraid to speak lest he say the wrong thing. The implications hung in the air like black smoke. She'd been tracking a rapist.

"A particularly heinous serial rapist," Cheyenne went on in that empty tone that tore at his heart. "He found me first. In my garage. He'd been stalking me. He laughed about that during the—" She stopped, started again. "I was chasing him. He was watching me, waiting for a chance to get me alone."

Trace shut his eyes against the despair in her voice. He knew. She didn't have to tell him that she'd been a victim. Everything he knew about her came to mind. Her fear of the dark, her defensiveness, her terror in a closed garage, the distrust.

"He raped you."

She nodded but her gaze never met his. A flush of shame darkened her olive skin.

"For . . . hours. I was in my own garage. Three steps and I would have been safe inside. But he'd locked the garage door down tight." Her hand went to her throat. "I couldn't get away. I couldn't reach my gun. But after—after a while he got careless. He thought he'd gained total control. In a way, he had. I was—I pleaded—I was . . . broken. I would have done anything he

said at that point. And I would have done anything to escape."

The dark eyes she lifted were filled with guilt
and devastation.

God, give me strength.

Anger such as he'd never known flooded
through Trace. Anger toward a man filled with
so much evil that he could do such a thing.

"My service weapon was under the car seat. I
kept reaching for it. Finally . . ." She squeezed
her eyelids tight. "I don't remember pulling the
trigger. But I remember the shock on his face
and the last breath he took. I was glad when he
went still and silent." She made a tiny sound of
distress. "What kind of person is glad when a
man is dead?"

Trace didn't answer, but his fingers stroked
the top of her hand over and over and over.

Cheyenne tried to draw comfort from Trace's
tenderness, but she was afraid to need him too
much. He'd be gone forever after tonight. So
would she.

Her stomach pitched. She hated thinking
about those hours alone with Dwight Hector,
but Trace had deserved to know and she had
needed to tell him. Now he would understand
why she could not let him love her. She was
defiled, unlovable, ruined.

A thousand times she'd wished she hadn't

gone into the bar after work. If she hadn't, she would still have been wearing the revolver in the shoulder holster. Her mind would have been perfectly clear. She would have seen the signs that someone was in her garage. She could have arrested Hector and avoided the entire incident.

She rubbed at the ache forming inside her forehead. "As a trained professional, I should have been able to prevent everything that happened that night."

"Whoa. Hold it right there."

The anger in Trace stopped her cold.

Carefully, she withdrew her fingers from beneath his and pushed away from the table. "I'll understand if you want to leave now."

"I'm not going anywhere."

She'd expected this. The compassionate vet would feel duty-bound to tend the wounded. "Don't worry about me. I'll be all right. Tomorrow I'm leaving Redemption. You can forget about me."

"Not going to happen."

"You're such a good man, Trace. Decent and good and a real Christian. Far too good for someone like me. I killed a man and he killed a part of me that I can't get back. I'll never be the person I was before."

"No one expects you to be. You're you. A strong, amazing woman with the compassion to

278

help someone like Emma. Don't sell yourself short."

But she felt worthless.

"I thought God had taken all of it away," she admitted. "Until the night you witnessed the flashback, I had been sleeping with the lights off and hadn't had a nightmare. I'd begun to believe healing was possible, but now—"

"With God in your corner, you will get better. When Pamela died, I thought I'd never breathe again. I didn't even want to, but I did. And eventually, with God's help and the support of my family, the guilt and sorrow disappeared."

He tenderly took both her hands and drew her slowly toward him. "Let me be here for you, Cheyenne. Don't push me away."

Inwardly, she battled. Was he feeling pity or love? Did he care for her? Or only care about her?

She shook her head, afraid to believe anything good at this point. "Don't be kind, Trace. I can't handle it tonight. You can't possibly want me now that you know."

"Stop it, Cheyenne." The hard edge in his tone shocked her. "If you don't want me, that's one thing, but don't deny my feelings for you. They're real." He tapped his chest. "My heart hurts for what happened to you. I hate it. I love you so much I'm bleeding inside to know what you went through and I wasn't there to protect you. But get this fact through your hard head. The rape does not change my love for you."

Stunned, moved, touched, she opened her mouth to speak, but Trace stopped her with a finger to her lips.

"Don't talk. Don't say a word until I'm finished. You had a right, even a responsibility to do your job as a police officer. You had a right to be in your own car, in your own garage. You had every right to defend yourself. The rapist made the choice. Not you. You had a right and he did not. His death was his fault, not yours. You saved someone else from suffering the hell you endured."

Cheyenne clung to every word. She had said those things to Emma not ten minutes ago. And she'd meant them. No man had a right to hurt a woman, in any manner.

Hope, like a broken-winged bird, flapped and fluttered, trying to rise and fly.

If they had any chance at all, she had to clear the air of everything. "I'd had a few drinks. The news media blamed me for everything. They said I was too cool, too collected, cold-blooded."

"But you weren't. There isn't a cold-blooded cell in your body."

Trace was right. The media didn't understand. They'd distorted everything and she'd bought in to their frenzy, taking the blame, accepting the humiliation as her due. But the light was beginning to dawn inside Cheyenne Rhodes.

"The only way I could cope was to detach before I came completely unraveled. I was going crazy inside."

"You were a news story. They didn't know you at all. But I know you. And I love you." He kissed her temple, his lips tickling against her hair. "If you'll let me, with God's help, I'll be the man you need."

"What if I have flashbacks? What if I can't be the woman *you* need?" Disappointing him was her greatest fear, but, oh, she longed to hear him say she wouldn't be a failure as a woman.

"You already are the woman I need. Don't you see? Since Pamela died, I've been half a man, living in limbo. Then you arrived with your puppies and pretty face and I became whole again. I need you, Cheyenne. What happened to you infuriates me more than I can ever show, and I will spend the rest of my life showing you how a real man treats a woman—with respect and tenderness."

"I already know that about you."

"Then know this, too. I will do whatever it takes to help you feel safe and lovable again. If it takes godly counseling, prayer, time, patience, whatever you need, you'll have it."

G. I. Jack's words about coming into God's marvelous light opened in Cheyenne's mind.

Before she could heal, she had to release the darkness.

Accepting the truth, for only the truth could set her free, she cupped his face in her hands and gazed deeply into the purest blue eyes. The love radiating from Trace washed through her in warm, purging, purifying waves.

And at long last, Cheyenne released the darkness and embraced the light.

Epilogue

Music rocked the community center, and the smell of spaghetti and garlic bread made more than one belly growl. A huge crowd milled around inside and outside the building.

Cheyenne sat at a small table at the entrance, collecting donations for the fundraiser. Trace, with his charm and popularity, moved among the townsfolk, urging additional support for the women's shelter to be built.

Six months had passed since the night Ray Madden had broken down her door and Trace Bowman had broken down her defenses. Since then, she and Trace had become a team, at the clinic, in community service and personally. Her life had taken a complete turn from the broken, confused woman she'd been the day she'd driven across the river bridge and entered Redemption.

Renewed and deepened trust in God had done that for her. God and the love of a good man.

True to his word, Trace hadn't rushed her. Together they'd sought Christian counseling and slowly built a relationship based on honesty and trust and God's Word. More and more each day, Trace Bowman became the man she needed and she believed with all her heart, she was becoming the woman he and Zoey needed.

The thought gave her immeasurable joy.

Trace, deep in conversation with a wealthy oil man, glanced across the room and caught her eye, giving a thumbs-up. Happiness expanded in her chest.

"You're looking mighty pleased, Miss Cheyenne." G. I. Jack pulled a hundred dollars from his breast pocket and plunked the bill on the table. She'd learned not to be surprised at anything about her two favorite senior gentlemen.

"Happy as a hog in a mud wallow," she said, and waited for him to grin at the phrase.

"One of these days you're gonna make a country girl," he said. "Where's our Zoey?"

Cheyenne gestured toward the long buffet line. "With Toby and some friends. They're helping Kitty and the others serve."

Kitty, Emma and seven women who regularly attended Cheyenne's library meetings worked tirelessly in the kitchen and serving line. Emma had come a long way since that awful night. She had completed her GED and was working part-time at the courthouse, stunned by how good she was at office work. Ray Madden had disappeared from Redemption, though Emma was convinced he'd return. But now she had friends and the self-confidence to stand strong.

"I daresay half the town has turned out for the occasion," Popbottle Jones said, adjusting an outdated tie. "In fact, I believe I spy a dear friend. Will the two of you excuse me, please?"

With a courtly bow, Popbottle Jones stood straight and tall, slicked both hands over his hair and walked with purpose toward one of the long, cloth-covered buffet tables. Annie Markham was setting a plate of spaghetti and salad in front of an older woman.

"Who is the lady with Annie and her kids?" she asked.

G. I. Jack watched his business partner with a speculative eye. "Miss Lydia Hawkins. She doesn't get out much these days. Bad health."

"I'm sorry to hear that."

"She's a fine woman. A prayer warrior." He turned to gaze down at Cheyenne. "You were on her list."

"Me?" At his nod, Cheyenne marveled. A

woman she didn't know had prayed for her. Maybe that was the "magic" of Redemption. People cared for strangers and friends alike. They prayed one for another, as the Bible said to do.

"Maybe you could return the favor," he said softly. "Annie, too. She's had a rough go of things even though she never lets on."

"I will." Giving back felt good, whether in prayer, in her weekly counseling sessions in the library, or in helping raise funds for the shelter. "Popbottle seems quite interested in Miss Lydia."

"I reckon you could say that."

He didn't elaborate, but Cheyenne heard the tone. "I want to meet her. Will you take over for me here?"

"Be dee-lighted to." He slid into her vacated chair. "You just watch and see. I'll harass more money out of these skinflints than you can shake a stick at."

Grinning, Cheyenne patted his shoulder and wound her way through the crowd, stopping often. Many of these people were her friends now. As she moved, she searched for Trace, wanting him by her side.

The band eased into a soft instrumental number as she reached Lydia Hawkins' table. Popbottle Jones made the introductions.

Not knowing how to offer gratitude for prayer,

Cheyenne sat down with the small party for a short chat. "Thank you for being here tonight."

"We've needed a shelter in Redemption for a long time," Annie said with a sad expression that made Cheyenne wonder.

Just then Trace appeared, his focus aimed at Cheyenne. Her pulse did a happy dance against her collarbone. She smiled up into his beloved face.

He tugged on her hand and she rose to meet him.

"You're needed outside for a moment."

"I am?" With a little wave to the guests, she let him draw her through the crowd and out the back way. The night was dark and the alley was empty.

Cheyenne gazed around, bewildered. "What's out here?"

Trace grinned. "You and me."

"But you said I was needed out here."

"You are. I needed to be alone with you for a few minutes."

"Oh, Trace." She melted. "Thank you."

"For what?"

"Everything. For bringing me out here. For loving me the way you do. For being exactly the man I need."

Strong arms pulled her closer until she felt the rise and fall of his chest and the steady beat of his heart. Trace Bowman, the Pollyanna vet, had the heart of a lion, a heart that beat for her.

The wonder of being loved by this man would never go away. Ever.

Before he'd come into her life, bringing God's love and light with him, she had been stumbling around in darkness, scared and alone.

She understood now what Kitty meant about Redemption drawing people in need. Redemption, or perhaps the spirit of faith and love and hope residing here, had taken her in all those months ago. And God in His great mercy had raised her from the depths of despair to peace and healing.

Trace tilted her chin and smiled. She smiled back.

"You're not afraid of the dark anymore."

"With you by my side, I'm not afraid of anything."

"When are you going to marry me?"

"The sooner, the better."

"That's the answer I've been waiting to hear."

And then his face descended and she welcomed him, at last, to be the woman she'd become, not the woman she'd been.

And the beauty of Trace's kiss was like a prayer, a fitting benediction on yesterday and a loving promise of what was yet to come.

Dear Reader,

I hope you have enjoyed *Finding Her Way Home,* the first book in my new series, REDEMPTION RIVER. I had a great time populating this fictional small town with quirky characters like Popbottle Jones and G. I. Jack. They, along with more of the townspeople, will return in each of the upcoming books.

In *Finding Her Way Home,* I chose a particularly difficult topic—violent rape. Even in today's more open society, rape is an uncomfortable subject. To make my heroine a realistic character, I researched heavily, read many blogs by rape survivors and explored the ways each of them worked toward healing. Those survivors with faith in God were especially helpful and they seemed to regain their emotional health faster than those without faith, though all struggled with many of the issues that plagued Cheyenne. I owe a debt of gratitude to all of those survivors for their willingness to share the most painful, life-changing episode of their lives.

On a lighter note, Trace and Cheyenne had an ongoing joke about Trace's "famous" recipe for popcorn. I thought you might enjoy a simple recipe such as the one mentioned in the book.

Chili-Cheese Popcorn Mix

1½ teaspoons chili powder
⅓ cup powdered cheese product
1 teaspoon garlic salt
⅛ teaspoon garlic cayenne pepper

Combine all ingredients in a small bowl. Makes ⅓ cup.

To use: Melt 2 tablespoons butter or margarine. Drizzle over 6 cups popped corn. Sprinkle with 1½ tablespoons mix and toss to coat.

Thank you again for reading, and don't forget to meet me again in Redemption River, where healing flows.

Linda Goodnight

QUESTIONS FOR DISCUSSION

1. Cheyenne believes she's come to Redemption by accident. Kitty tells her God leads needy people to the small town. Do you think such a thing is possible? Does God really lead people to do things? If your answer is yes, how has he led you?

2. Have you ever known someone who was a victim of a violent crime? How did the crime affect that person? How did he/she cope and recover?

3. Cheyenne was filled with a mix of shame, guilt and deep humiliation, all typical responses in a rape victim. Why do you think women react this way? Why would someone blame herself for such a crime? Is rape ever the fault of the victim?

4. Cheyenne's friends and family were uncomfortable with her after the rape, another common reaction. Why do you think this happens? In what ways could a friend or family member be a comfort and help to a rape victim?

5. Trace's motto was "Today is the best day ever" but Cheyenne's was "Nobody does something for nothing." Which of these is closest to the way you feel? If you had a personal motto, what would it be?

6. Trace has seen his share of tragedy and yet he is emotionally healthy. Why do you think this is so? Do you think his relationship with God had anything to do with his ability to heal after his wife died? Have you ever faced a tragedy and found strength and healing through your faith?

7. When Cheyenne first arrives in town, she misjudges the two old Dumpster-divers. Have you ever misjudged someone because of appearance? What does scripture say about how God judges us?

8. The town of Redemption is populated by a number of interesting characters. Who was your favorite secondary character? Why?

9. The well at Town Square is engraved with scripture. What was it? How did it play a part in Cheyenne's character growth? Why do you think the other characters kept asking her if she had seen the well?

10. Trace's daughter Zoey is blind, but Popbottle Jones and G. I. Jack said she had vision. What did they mean? Contrast Zoey's type of darkness with Cheyenne's.

11. The Bible says "God is light and in Him is no darkness." What does this mean? How could this apply to the story and to Cheyenne's emotional darkness?

12. Is it scripturally acceptable for a woman like Emma Madden to leave her abusive spouse? Discuss the various views on this and find scripture to back up your opinion.

13. Because she'd had a few drinks the night of the rape, Cheyenne is certain God must be angry with her. Do you think God "punishes" our mistakes? Or do you think we sometimes punish ourselves instead? Is there any scripture to support your opinion?

14. Trace tells Zoey that God has a perfect plan for each of us. Do you believe that? Can you find the scripture that supports this?

15. Do you believe God has a plan for your life? What is it? How can a person know God's perfect plan?

LINDA GOODNIGHT

Winner of a RITA® Award for excellence in inspirational fiction, Linda Goodnight has also won the Booksellers' Best, ACFW Book of the Year, and a Reviewers' Choice Award from *RT Book Reviews*. Linda has appeared on the Christian bestseller list and her romance novels have been translated into more than a dozen languages. Active in orphan ministry, this former nurse and teacher enjoys writing fiction that carries a message of hope and light in a sometimes dark world. She and her husband, Gene, live in Oklahoma. Readers can write to her at linda@lindagoodnight.com, or c/o Steeple Hill Books, 233 Broadway, Suite 1001, New York, NY 10279.

Center Point Publishing
600 Brooks Road ● PO Box 1
Thorndike ME 04986-0001 USA

(207) 568-3717

US & Canada:
1 800 929-9108
www.centerpointlargeprint.com